THE LLANGOLLEN KILLINGS

A Snowdonia Murder Mystery

DI Ruth Hunter Crime Thriller #19

SIMON MCCLEAVE

STAMFORD
PUBLISHING

THE LLANGOLLEN KILLINGS

By Simon McCleave

A DI Ruth Hunter Crime Thriller
Book 19

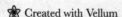 Created with Vellum

BOOKS BY SIMON McCLEAVE

THE DI RUTH HUNTER SERIES

#1 The Snowdonia Killings

#2. The Harlech Beach Killings

#3. The Dee Valley Killings

#4. The Devil's Cliff Killings

#5. The Berwyn River Killings

#6. The White Forest Killings

#7. The Solace Farm Killings

#8. The Menai Bridge Killings

#9. The Conway Harbour Killings

#10. The River Seine Killings

#11. The Lake Vyrnwy Killings

#12. The Chirk Castle Killings

#13. The Portmeirion Killings

#14. The Llandudno Pier Killings

#15. The Denbigh Asylum Killings

#16. The Wrexham Killings

#17. The Colwyn Bay Killings

#18. The Chester Killings

#19. The Llangollen Killings

THE DC RUTH HUNTER MURDER CASE SERIES

#1. Diary of a War Crime

#2. The Razor Gang Murder

#3. An Imitation of Darkness

#4. This is London, SE15

THE ANGLESEY SERIES - DI LAURA HART

#1. The Dark Tide

#2. In Too Deep

#3. Blood on the Shore

#4. The Drowning Isle

#5. Dead in the Water

Your FREE book is waiting for you now!

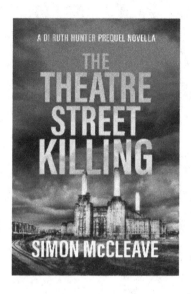

Get your FREE copy of the prequel to
the DI Ruth Hunter Series NOW
http://www.simonmccleave.com/vip-email-club
and join my VIP Email Club

*For the beautiful Sophie Pemberton
who was taken from us too soon*

You will be missed so much xx

Prologue

HELMAND PROVINCE, AFGHANISTAN
AUGUST 2007

IT WAS DAWN. The first platoon of the Welsh Guards had been ordered to recce an area for a new forward operating base – FOB. From there, they were going to protect the main road heading south. In recent months, British Army convoys had been ambushed or attacked by the Taliban with improvised explosive devices. It was the Welsh Guards' job to secure the village of Bakhsh Abad and the surrounding area, flushing out and killing any insurgents as they went.

The conflict in Afghanistan had been raging since 2001 when an international military coalition invaded in direct response to the September 11 attacks. The Taliban regime had been expelled from most of the major population centres by troops. By 2007, Taliban insurgents had been waging guerrilla warfare against coalition troops, managing to retake large chunks of Afghanistan back. The British Army in Helmand Province were attempting a 'clear and hold' strategy for all villages and towns with varying success.

Sergeant Gary Williams stopped and waited for the rest of his platoon to catch up. They'd already covered three miles. The temperature had been rising slowly as the tangerine sun burned away the early morning clouds. That was the frustrating thing about Helmand. The days were burning hot and the nights unbearably cold.

In his late 20s, Gary was tall and muscular with a shaved head and dark stubble. On the top of his right arm he had a red Welsh Dragon tattoo. Taking out his L12A1 Avimo self-focusing binoculars, he scanned the area ahead. The sandy limestone ground had cracked in dark jagged patterns, and the blackened shape of a lorry lay over to their right. It was still smouldering, and the air smelled of burning metal and oil. Beyond that was a line of one-storey shops and buildings of a village which seemed to be deserted.

The Welsh Guards were two months into their tour. Gary could see the psychological damage that the fierce fighting had inflicted on his men. It was only a week since Lance Corporal Lee Jenkins had the back of his head blown off. Jenkins had gone up a ladder to a lookout position at their base after reports of several 'flip flops' being spotted approaching. 'Flip flops' was army slang for the Taliban soldiers. After an hour, it was assumed to be a false alarm. A couple of privates had started to discuss what they were having for tea. Jenkins sat up and looked over to join in with the conversation. There was the sudden distant sound of a high-velocity rifle. Before he could react, his helmet flew off as the back of his head exploded. Even though they'd rushed him to the medics, he died on the helicopter back to Camp Bastion.

Gary looked back and saw two privates approaching slowly. Ian Bellamy and Aaron Jenkins, Lee Jenkins' younger brother. Gary was worried about Aaron since the death of his brother. He had flatly refused to take any compassionate leave, which could have been arranged after Lee's death. Aaron seemed hell-bent on getting some kind of revenge for his brother which made him dangerous to everyone in the platoon.

'Anything, sarge?' Aaron asked, drawing breath.

Gary shook his head. He took the binoculars again. This time he spotted movement over by an abandoned petrol station.

'Shit,' he muttered under his breath as his pulse quickened.

Two men were hiding behind a battered pickup truck. It looked like they had a belt-fed XM250 machine gun on a tripod.

And it was aimed in their direction.

This is not good.

The British Army were getting wise to the Taliban's tactics. They knew that the British troops' smaller calibre firearms were ineffective at distance. So the Taliban employed the use of heavy machine guns and rocket-propelled grenades rather than engage in close range fire fights.

'What is it, sarge?' Aaron asked.

Gary could feel the muscles in his stomach tighten and he handed over the binoculars. Aaron peered through them at the buildings and nodded to signal that he'd seen the men too. 'Shit,' he hissed.

Gary knew that the two men with the machine gun wouldn't be on their own.

It was an ambush.

Gary's heart was now pounding. He turned around and silently signalled for the whole platoon to get down and take cover.

Suddenly the air seemed to explode with noise as Taliban fighters opened fire on them from various locations.

Diving to the ground, Gary tried to make himself as low and as small as possible. The rocky terrain dissolved in clouds of dust as if being pelted by hailstones. A tracer whizzed overhead.

'Get down!' he yelled.

Squinting for signs of muzzle flashes, Gary calculated that the gunfire seemed to be coming from at least half a dozen of the buildings.

Grabbing his binoculars, he scanned the area again and saw a Taliban fighter on the roof of the garage with a Soviet made RPG-7. It was their weapon of choice in situations like this.

'RPG!' Gary bellowed. 'Take cover.' Then he glanced over at Private Wayne Davies, the platoon's radio telephone operator – RTO. 'Davies, call in air support now,' he yelled.

'I'm on it, sarge.' Grabbing the satellite radio, Davies went to work.

An RPG landed on the ground about twenty yards away with a thunderous explosion. Gary was showered with fragments of dirt but luckily no shrapnel.

Thank fuck he's a crap shot, he thought as he blew out his cheeks.

However, they were pinned down, and unless air support arrived the situation was only going to get worse.

The sporadic gunfire continued for several more minutes.

Then a deep roar from the air above. Gary knew exactly what it was as he glanced up hopefully.

A British Harrier GR9 jet.

He watched as two 540lb laser-guided bombs whistled towards the low buildings in the distance.

BOOM!

The horizon disappeared in a flash of flames and smoke. The noise and force of the blast was colossal. The whole ground shook.

All that was left of the buildings was rubble, fire and smoke.

Someone let off a burst of gunfire from behind him.

'Cease fire!' Gary shouted angrily. It was clear that a dozen or so Taliban soldiers had been blown to pieces. No one could have survived that blast.

With another signal, Gary got to his feet and beckoned the patrol forward. They needed to secure the village and the surrounding area.

He spotted that Aaron had a nasty shrapnel cut on his face which was bleeding.

'You okay?' Gary asked him. 'We need to get that cleaned up.'

Aaron smiled and wiped the blood from his face. 'Just a scratch. I'm fine.'

The patrol continued to make their way towards the village.

'You smell that?' Aaron said in an American accent. 'You smell that? I love the smell of roasted Taliban in the morning. Smells like victory.' There were a few laughs at Aaron's impression of one of the characters from the film *Apocalypse Now*.

Gary scanned the burning buildings as they got closer. The air was thick with acrid smoke. Looking down, he checked that the safety was still off on his SA80 rifle. He wasn't taking any chances.

Suddenly a bearded man in his 40s came from behind the petrol station. He looked terrified. He had his hands up in the air as he babbled nervously at them in the Farsi dialect.

Raising his rifle, Gary shouted, 'Get down on the ground now!'

Even though the man was clearly unarmed and frightened, there had been incidents where Taliban soldiers had pretended to surrender before setting off a suicide bomb.

Looking at the man's hands, Gary could see there was no trigger device. He might well be a villager who hadn't managed to escape when the Taliban had arrived.

CRACK! CRACK!

Two bullets hammered into the man's torso.

What the fuck?

Clutching at his chest, the man gave Gary a bewildered look as he crumpled to the ground.

'For fuck's sake!' Gary thundered as he looked around.

Aaron's rifle was lodged into the nook of his shoulder and the end of the barrel was smoking.

'What the hell are you doing?' Gary yelled.

'We're here to kill the Taliban, sarge,' Aaron said with a nonchalant shrug.

The man was still groaning on the ground in pain as Private Bellamy went over to him.

Gary fixed Aaron with a glare. 'He was unarmed. He had his hands up. Shooting him is a fucking war crime, you idiot!'

Aaron pulled an angry face. 'Everyone here is Taliban as far as I'm concerned. And we need to wipe them off the face of the planet.'

'No explosives, sarge,' Bellamy confirmed.

Gary shook his head. This was not good. He could feel his anxiety growing. He could feel the whole platoon waiting to see how he was going to react to Aaron shooting an innocent man who posed no threat to life and was surrendering.

The man was still writhing in pain.

'Jesus Christ,' Gary growled under his breath as he tried to gather his thoughts.

The tension was growing.

Taking out his Glock 17 handgun from its holster, Gary moved swiftly over to the injured man and shot him between his eyes.

Then he looked at the platoon who appeared shocked by what he'd done. 'Right, this man came from over there. We repeatedly commanded him to stop but he didn't. We feared that he might have been carrying explosives so we shot him. Anyone have a problem with that?' he asked forcefully.

Silence.

Gary glared at Aaron. 'And when we get back to base, you're going on immediate compassionate leave. Understood?'

Aaron nodded but didn't look remotely remorseful for what he'd done.

Private Davies caught Gary's eye and pointed. 'Sarge?'

About thirty yards away, a boy who was about ten years old was watching them from the rubble of the petrol station.

'Shit!' Gary hissed, and then broke into a run after him. Davies followed.

The boy turned, sprinted and disappeared.

Gary and Davies clambered over the smoking rubble, avoiding small patches of flames.

As they ran onto the petrol station concourse, Gary

realised that the boy had completely disappeared. And he could be hiding anywhere.

The boy was also witness to him shooting an injured innocent man in cold blood.

1

Bangor-On-Dee

AUGUST 2021

IT WAS a perfect summer's evening. The sun had started to sink in the sky and was turning the clouds a stunning hue of pink and purple.

DI Ruth Hunter popped a cigarette into her mouth, shielded it with her other hand from the gentle summer breeze, and lit it. Sitting back, she took a long drag and then let out the plume of smoke with a satisfied sigh.

The bells from the nearby St Dunawd's Church chimed to signal that it was eight o'clock.

'Wine?' called a voice. It was Ruth's partner, Sarah.

'Pope, silly hat,' Ruth replied with a grin.

Looking up at the sky, Ruth couldn't remember feeling this peaceful for a long time. The past few weeks at Llan-castell CID had been relatively quiet, although no one dared use the dreaded *Q word*. The only thing hanging over her was the ongoing battle to adopt Daniel, the eleven-year-old boy they were looking after on a temporary foster licence.

Five weeks earlier, the paperwork for Daniel's permanent adoption had been signed. However, he had been kidnapped by Nina Taylor, a female serial killer, before being dramatically rescued up on the North Wales coast at the Great Orme. Social services had put a hold on Ruth and Sarah's permanent adoption of Daniel. Nina Taylor had targeted him as a way of getting to Ruth. Therefore social services needed to do a thorough review and risk assessment to see if Ruth's job could ever put Daniel in danger again. Waiting for them to reach their conclusion was making Ruth and Sarah jittery.

Sarah approached with two large glasses of rosé and handed one to Ruth. 'Here you go, chuck.'

'Since when did rosé become the nation's wine of choice?' Ruth said, thinking out loud.

Sarah shrugged. 'I can't remember.'

'When I was a kid, rosé was cheap, nasty wine that we drank in our early teens.'

'Mateus Rosé,' Sarah said with a reminiscent nod.

'Now it's the fashionable thing to drink,' Ruth said.

'Jeremy Clarkson was photographed drinking it,' Sarah pointed out, 'although he did refer to it as *lady petrol*.'

'That's because he's a mysogynistic neanderthal,' Ruth joked.

Sarah looked over at her thoughtfully. 'We should take Daniel away before he goes back school.'

Ruth nodded. 'We should, if he feels up to it.'

Their plans for a summer holiday had been shelved as they wanted to make sure that Daniel had fully recovered from his traumatic ordeal in July. He'd had a few nights where he'd suffered terrible nightmares so they were keeping a close eye on him.

'It'll be his first time abroad,' Sarah stated, and then sat back and sipped her wine. 'Where would we go?'

'My first holiday was a package to Santo Tomas in Menorca. Mum, dad and me and my brother. 1985. I remember snogging this sixteen-year-old boy called Danny White in Nelson's nightclub. He claimed he'd been to Live Aid. He had white espadrilles and this grey flecked jacket with the sleeves rolled up. I thought he looked a bit like Don Johnson from *Miami Vice*.'

'Did he?'

'No, he looked more like Gripper Stebson from *Grange Hill*.'

Sarah laughed, took a long sip of wine and then looked over at Ruth. 'I had a message from Susannah earlier,' she said gently.

Ruth instantly felt a pang of anxiety. Susannah was their social worker who was working with them on their possible adoption of Daniel. She had been incredibly supportive throughout the process and Ruth and Sarah could see how good she was at her job. There was no resentment at her recommendation that the adoption process be put on hold after Daniel's kidnapping. In fact Ruth would have been concerned if there hadn't been some kind of assessment of Daniel and possible risks in the future.

'What did she say?' Ruth asked apprehensively.

'She's going to pop in this week sometime to update us on the adoption and to see how Daniel is getting on.'

'Fair enough,' Ruth replied as she dragged on her cigarette again. The whole thing seemed to weigh heavily on her.

'You're not supposed to be smoking,' called a voice.

Ruth looked up and saw Daniel looking down from his bedroom window. She had promised him that she would stop smoking. In fact she had managed to quit for a couple of months. But after she had been shot and almost died, Ruth had decided that life was too short not to do the things that she loved. And, however ridiculous it might seem, smoking was one of her favourite things so she wasn't going to stop.

'Sorry,' Ruth said with an innocent shrug. 'It's only my second one today.' It was actually her tenth but she wasn't going to admit that.

Daniel shook his head in a slightly jokey way.

Sarah got up from her seat. 'I'll come up and tuck you in.'

Daniel pulled a face. 'I don't need tucking in. I'm eleven.'

'Yeah, well I'm coming up anyway,' she laughed.

'Night, Daniel,' Ruth said as she looked up.

'Night.' Then he wagged his finger at her. 'And no more ciggies.'

Ruth nodded with a smile. 'I promise.'

Daniel closed the window.

Ruth then pulled an apologetic face at Sarah. 'Now I feel really guilty.'

'Good,' Sarah said with a raise of her eyebrow as she turned and headed inside.

Reaching for her phone, Ruth went to check that there hadn't been any calls or emails from work.

A BBC News story popped up on her feed.

SHIPMENT OF GUNS *seized at Liverpool Docks*

BORDER FORCE OFFICERS *have uncovered what is believed to be the biggest haul of guns at Liverpool Docks this afternoon. Over sixty firearms were discovered hidden in an articulated lorry arriving from Ireland. Several lethal automatic firearms were discovered in secret panels along with a dozen SIG Sauer P226 handguns.*

In a joint operation between Border Forces, the National Crime Agency (NCA) and Merseyside Police Anti-gang unit, the haul is believed to be the largest ever seizure of lethal firearms at a UK port.

Chapter 2

It was Monday afternoon, and retired army Major Leonard Nevin and his wife Mary were taking their grandchildren, Daisy and Jack, on a trip to the Llangollen Steam Railway. It was a treat during their summer holidays. The journey on the heritage railway ran for over ten miles, following the River Dee through the Dee Valley to Corwen with spectacular views of Snowdonia National Park.

Now in his late 70s, Leonard could remember the old steam trains when he was growing up. He thought it was the 'Golden Age of Steam'. He and his friend Nigel Spencer used to go train spotting as boys around North Wales and the North West of England. Now in his retirement, Leonard had ridden many of the heritage steam railways in the UK. From the North Yorkshire Moors Railway to the East Somerset Railway, he loved them all. But he had a soft spot for Llangollen as this is where he grew up. He knew that Mary indulged him in his passion rather than shared it.

As Leonard, Mary and his grandchildren boarded the train, he felt an immense sense of nostalgic pride and excitement. The station at Llangollen had retained its Victorian design and the vintage colour scheme of the Great Western Railway had been used throughout. It was like stepping back into the late 1950s, Leonard thought. The familiar clunk of the heavy carriage doors. The redolent smell of the fabric seats and wooden panels.

Ah, bliss, he thought. *And it's such a beautiful summer's day too.*

They settled themselves into their seats, which were covered in a dark red material and a gold pattern of interlocking, elongated circles. They heard the whistle of the platform guard to signal that they were pulling out of the station. Then the beautiful toot of the iconic pannier tank engine that had been built in Glasgow back in 1930. Leonard felt like he'd been transported back in time.

'I once travelled on the Flying Scotsman,' Leonard proudly informed his grandchildren.

Mary smiled and rolled her eyes. 'Leo, they don't have a clue what the Flying Scotsman is.'

Jack frowned. 'Is he a superhero, Grandad?' he enquired innocently.

Leonard and Mary laughed.

'No. The Flying Scotsman was the most famous train in the whole world,' Leonard stated, waxing lyrical. 'It ran from Edinburgh to London on the East Coast Main Line. It weighed over a hundred tonnes and was the first train ever to go over 100mph.'

He could see they were all suitably underwhelmed. Everyone in his family was underwhelmed or plain bored by his obsession with all things steam.

Jack, who had just turned twelve, pulled out his iPhone, held it up and started to record.

Leonard smiled. 'Ooh. Are you making a documentary, Jack?'

Jack looked confused. 'I'm making a video for Tik Tok, Grandad,' he explained in a slightly patronising tone.

Leonard looked over at Mary who gave him a wry smile.

'Tik Tok?' he asked, raising his eyebrow.

'I bet you've never been on Tik Tok before, have you Leo?' she joked, teasing him.

'I really haven't,' he chortled.

Out of the corner of his eye, Leonard spotted something in a field in the distance. Two figures were standing talking to each other. They seemed to be animated as if arguing and shoving each other.

What's going on over there? he wondered as he stared out at them.

The train was going slowly enough for him to see them for several seconds.

Suddenly, one of the figures lifted their hand. They were holding something.

It looked like a gun.

In fact to Leonard's trained eye it looked like a submachine gun.

What the hell is going on?

Leonard stood up abruptly and went to the window so that he could see what was happening.

Then the distinct flash of a muzzle.

'Good God,' he muttered in shock.

Mary got up to see what he was looking at.

Grabbing his mobile phone, Leonard dialled 999. 'Police please …'

Chapter 3

It was a baking hot bank holiday afternoon and Ruth and Sarah had invited a few people over for a barbeque. The air was still, and thick with the smells of barbeque coals.

Detective Sergeant Nick Evans, Ruth's right-hand man at Llancastell CID, stood over on the patio with his wife Amanda. Their daughter Megan, Ruth's goddaughter, was toddling around on the lawn in a pink sunhat, dress and sunglasses. Ruth's daughter, Ella, mid-20s, and Daniel were busy throwing a ball for Megan to try and catch.

Ruth finished her wine and wondered if she should go and get a top up. She was trying to pace herself. Sarah was taking charge of putting food on the barbeque and taking orders of what everyone wanted. They had spent the morning preparing. A table with condiments, salad, napkins and paper plates was on the far side of the patio.

The Bluetooth speaker was playing Ruth's Ibiza chilled playlist via Spotify – *Blue Chair* by *Morcheeba.*

Wow, it doesn't really get any better than this does it? she thought to herself contentedly. *Perfect weather, all the people I love. I feel like the luckiest woman in the world right now.*

Strolling across the patio, she headed for the door that led into the kitchen.

'Ruth?' called a voice.

It was Sarah who was now decked out in a black chef's apron that had a heart shape with the rainbow colours of the pride flag and *Lesbian Chefs Rock, bitch!* printed in white lettering.

'Yes?'

'Could you be a doll and grab the cheese slices from the fridge for me?' she called over.

'I'm on it,' Ruth replied with a smile. For a moment, she looked at Sarah in her apron with her vintage Boho sunglasses and brown arms.

She really is so attractive.

Sarah sipped her wine and then let out a cackling laugh at something Nick had said to her – something inappropriate no doubt.

AND I REALLY DO LOVE THAT *woman*, Ruth thought as she turned and went back inside.

Standing by the fridge was DC Georgie Wild. In the past six months, Ruth and Georgie had become close. Georgie was pregnant after sleeping with a young journalist who had then been killed in a road traffic accident. Georgie had decided to keep the baby and so Ruth was doing everything she could to support her.

'Trying to keep cool?' Ruth asked as she went in.

Georgie turned and smiled at her. 'If I could, I'd just sit in your fridge.'

'Help yourself,' Ruth joked. She vaguely remembered what it was like to be six months pregnant and starting to feel uncomfortable.

Georgie blew out her cheeks as she took a bottle of sparkling mineral water out of the fridge and began to pour herself a drink.

Ruth gave her a concerned look. 'Are you feeling okay?'

'Just a bit woozy,' Georgie admitted. 'No one told me that I was going to be this tired.'

Ruth gestured to the stairs. 'Go upstairs and have a nap on our bed. Seriously.'

Georgie shook her head. 'I'm fine, honestly.'

Ruth gave her a look and then a half-smile. 'That's an order.'

'Oh right,' Georgie chortled. 'Thank you.'

Watching Georgie walk down the hallway, Ruth felt a maternal concern for her and the future. She would do everything she could to help her.

Grabbing a bottle of rosé from the fridge, Ruth poured herself a decent glass. She was desperate for a cigarette. It had been over an hour since she disappeared down the side alley on the far side of her house to have a sneaky smoke.

Her phone buzzed in her pocket.

Looking at the caller ID, she saw it was *Llancastell CID*.

Her heart sank. It was a Sunday afternoon so that meant it was something important. Or at least it had better be.

'DI Hunter?' she said as she answered.

'Boss?'

It was DC Dan French. He was part of the skeleton CID team working over the weekend.

'What's up, Dan?' she asked, but she knew he wasn't ringing her for a chat.

'We've got a possible murder over in Llangollen,' he explained. 'Suspect was shot in a field. We've got an eyewitness who saw it from the tourist steam train in Llangollen. We've got two uniformed patrols over there now, securing the crime scene and taking statements.'

Bloody hell!

'Right,' she said as she started to go into DI mode. There was no point getting annoyed about it. This was her job and someone had been killed. 'Tell uniform we'll be there in twenty minutes.'

'Sorry to ruin your Sunday, boss,' French apologised.

'Unfortunately we don't get to pick when people commit crimes,' Ruth said stoically. 'I'll see you later.'

Ruth ended the call and made her way out to the garden.

She caught Nick's eye and gave him an apologetic look. He nodded to indicate he knew what she meant. Then he leaned in and spoke to Amanda.

Ruth approached Sarah and gestured to her phone. 'I'm so sorry. I've got to go.'

Sarah looked disappointed, but nodded. It wasn't the first time a beautiful afternoon had been interrupted and it wouldn't be the last. 'I'll save you a sausage, shall I?'

Ruth went over and gave her a kiss. 'And a burger.'

Ruth and Nick made their way across the garden and down the hallway where Ruth grabbed her car keys.

They went out of the front door and headed for the car.

'That's the beauty of having an alcoholic deputy SIO,' Ruth quipped as she tossed the car keys to Nick. 'You can always drive.'

Nick laughed. 'And you can drink and smoke.'

'Sounds like the perfect combo,' Ruth said as she opened the passenger door and got in. As she settled herself into the passenger seat and put on her seatbelt, she had a thought and looked over at Nick. 'Oh God, do I smell of booze?'

He reached into his pocket, pulled out a packet of chewing gum and handed it to her. 'Here you go.'

Ruth smiled. 'Right. I'll take that as a yes then?' she joked.

Chapter 4

Twenty minutes later, Ruth and Nick reached the outskirts of Llangollen, a town situated on the River Dee which was very popular with tourists visiting North Wales, especially in the summer months. It stood between Wrexham and Snowdonia National Park, on the edge of the Berwyn Mountains and the Dee Valley section of the Clywdian Range. Its name derived from the Welsh for 'a religious settlement' – *Llan* – and Saint Collen, a 7th century monk who first established a church beside the River Dee.

As it was the height of summer, the town was packed. Nick slowed the car in the traffic as they turned right across the 14th century stone bridge that crossed both the river and the trainline.

Looking left, Nick moved his Ray-Ban Wayfarer sunglasses down the bridge of his nose. 'In my late teens, we used to come here in the summer. We'd go on a pub crawl. And then my party trick was to jump fully clothed off that bridge into the river.'

Ruth raised an eyebrow. 'That sounds very sensible,' she said sarcastically. 'How deep is it?'

'Depends. It fluctuates. I guess that was part of the thrill,' Nick explained as they came to a halt in the traffic. 'That far side was known as *Cesar's Side.* So my other party trick was to stand up on the wall of the bridge over the river and wait until there were tourists watching me. Then I'd jump in, hold my breath and swim under the bridge underwater. The tourists would all panic and think that I'd disappeared and drowned. My mates thought it was hilarious.'

'Oh yes, that is hilarious,' Ruth agreed dryly. 'What a shining example of maturity you were as a young man.'

'Oh, and I suppose you were squeaky clean,' Nick retorted with a grin. 'Throwing your knickers at Wham! and Duran Duran.'

'Oi, I never threw my knickers at anyone,' Ruth protested. 'Although I might have done if I'd been close enough to Shirlie Holliman.' She was referring to Wham's famous backing singer.

As the traffic cleared and they pulled forward onto the busy high street, Nick's eyes widened. 'You had a crush on Shirlie from Wham!?'

'Massive crush. I was gutted when I heard she was going out with Martin Kemp from Spandau Ballet.'

Nick laughed.

'It's not funny. The day Martin and Shirlie got married was a day that a little bit of me died inside.'

Nick shook his head with amusement.

Turning right onto the A5, they headed out of Llangollen towards where the shooting had been reported.

The Vale of Llangollen was spectacular in the summer sun. Swathes of green fields banked by rolling hills. It encompassed a stunning section of the famous Offa's Dyke Path, a 177-mile route that loosely followed the Wales-England border. Constructed by King Offa of Mercia in the 8th century, walkers from all around the world were drawn to its stunning scenery.

Nick turned the car to the right. There was a sign that read *Manor Farm*. They followed a bumpy track downhill towards an old farmhouse. Parked in the concrete yard were two yellow and blue marked patrol cars with *HEDDLU* printed on them. There was also a white scene of crime officer's van which had clearly just arrived with forensic officers.

'Here we go,' he said as he parked.

They got out and Ruth was immediately hit by the thick smell of silage. She assumed that the hot weather made 'the scents of the countryside' far worse. Nearby was an old red, mud-splattered Massey Ferguson tractor.

Scanning the area, Ruth spotted a couple of officers in luminous jackets standing in a field.

'I guess we're over there,' she said, gesturing as she saw a female police officer start to cordon off the field with blue and white evidence tape.

As they approached, Ruth could see that the first couple of SOCOs, in their white nitrile forensic suits, hats, masks and rubber boots, had already arrived. The uniformed sergeant, who had been first on scene, had clearly considered the area a serious crime scene.

A thickset uniformed officer with a ruddy face was on his phone. He hung up, saw them approaching and turned to greet them.

Ruth and Nick pulled out their warrant cards. 'DI Hunter and DS Evans, Llancastell CID.'

'Sergeant Edwards,' the officer said by way of an introduction. Ruth assumed that Edwards was local plod from Llangollen nick which she knew was a small rural police station.

'What have we got sergeant?' she asked.

'Victim is unidentified so far. Male, early 40s. Gunshot wounds to the chest, abdomen and legs,' Edwards explained and then pulled a face. 'Bit of a mess if I'm honest.'

Nick gestured to the farmhouse. 'Any idea who lives here?'

'The farm is registered to an Aaron Jenkins,' Edwards replied and looked over at the field. 'But at the moment, we haven't got anyone who can identify the victim or tell us if it's Aaron Jenkins over there.'

'Any eyewitnesses?' Ruth enquired.

Edwards looked down at his notebook. 'We've got a Leonard Nevin. He spotted the shooting from one of the heritage steam trains. He and his wife were taking their grandchildren on a trip.' He then pointed across the fields. 'The track runs across there.'

Nick rubbed his beard and then asked, 'And where is he now?'

'He seemed a bit shaken,' Edwards replied. 'I sent him, his wife and the kids home. He did inform me that he was a retired army Major. He seemed to think that was important.'

Ruth was confused. 'Any idea why?'

Edwards shook his head.

Ruth then gestured towards the field. 'Right, we'd better go and have a look.'

Ruth, Nick and Edwards made their way across the yard. The mud had baked hard in the summer sun and crunched a little under their feet as they walked.

The SOCOs were beginning to erect a white forensic tent to cover the victim's body. Another SOCO was crouched down taking photographs.

'Any sign of the pathologist yet?' Ruth asked as they went.

'No, ma'am. It's a bank holiday afternoon so it was difficult to track anyone down.'

As was standard now with any murder crime scene, they were handed white forensic suits, masks, hats and boots to wear before they could enter.

Looking up at the blazing sun, Ruth thought that it really wasn't the weather to be wearing a full forensic suit.

Taking a few slow strides, Ruth and Nick approached the body of the victim. He was lying on his back, dressed in a green plaid shirt and jeans. However, the shirt and jeans were now soaked in dark blood from what looked like multiple gunshot wounds.

The man had a dark beard and a tanned, weathered face. He had a deep scar running across the top of his right eyebrow and forehead.

Ruth crouched down to look closer. The man's jeans and black work boots were also covered in dried mud and dirt. If she had to guess, he worked outdoors and probably on the farm.

Nick, who was now crouched next to her, frowned. 'These gunshot wounds look like they were caused by a rifle or a handgun,' he observed. 'It's definitely not a shotgun wound.'

Ruth agreed. 'No, it's not.' A shotgun left a large messy wound from the hundreds of lead pellets that were packed into the cartridge. This man had five or six holes in his abdomen, his chest and legs. Ruth thought it was curious, because when they were called to a shooting at a farm or anywhere agricultural, the weapon nearly always turned out to be a shotgun. After all, it was incredibly easy to obtain a shotgun licence in rural areas such as North Wales. And it was also rare to see anyone with half a dozen gunshot wounds anywhere.

Ruth and Nick stood up. There wasn't much else they

could do until they got the results of a preliminary post-mortem and forensics.

Making their way back to a SOCO, they took off their forensic clothes and handed them back before rejoining Edwards.

'They're not shotgun wounds,' Ruth said.

'No,' Edwards agreed. 'I did think that myself.'

Before they could say anything else, a uniformed female police officer in her 30s came over. She was wearing blue forensic gloves.

'Sarge,' she said as she pointed to the farmhouse and then held up a clear evidence bag. Inside was a blue UK passport. 'We found this in a desk in the living room. It belongs to an Aaron Jenkins.'

Taking the bag carefully, Edwards opened the passport through the plastic so that he could see the photograph of Jenkins. Peering at the photo of a man in his early 40s, Edwards then turned it to show Ruth and Nick.

Despite the lack of a beard, it was definitely him.

'Yeah, looks like our victim to me,' Nick stated.

Ruth nodded in agreement. At least they now had a name and identity for their victim. And with his passport, they could get a decent amount of information in a short amount of time.

Ruth looked at Edwards. 'Our priority is to find Aaron's next of kin.'

The female police officer raised an eyebrow. 'Ma'am, there are definitely signs in the bedroom and bathroom of the farmhouse that a woman lives there.'

'Right, well we need to know who that is and make sure that she's safe.'

'There is something else,' the female officer said.

Ruth nodded. 'Go on.'

'There's an open gun cabinet in the living room,' she

explained, 'and whatever guns were in there, it's now completely empty.' She took out another evidence bag and held it up to show them. 'But we did find this in there.'

Inside the evidence bag was a clear plastic box of bullets with gold casings and copper-coloured tips. The label read – *9mm ammunition – Loose pack – x 200.*

Ruth gave Nick a look. She knew that 9mm ammunition was normally used in powerful handguns such as Glocks, or small automatic weapons. She wondered what the hell a farmer in North Wales was doing with ammunition like that.

Chapter 5

It was mid-afternoon and DC Jim Garrow was sitting quietly on one of the narrow wooden benches that lined the main corridor at Mold Crown Court. He was due to give evidence in the preliminary hearing of a murder trial dating back to April. The defendant, Lucy Morgan, had been found at the Pontcysyllte Aqueduct claiming to have amnesia on the night that her mother, Lynne Morgan, was brutally murdered at her home in Wrexham. Garrow and DC Dan French's investigation had eventually discovered that Lucy had slashed her mother's throat after a heated argument and then faked her amnesia to cover her tracks.

However, the major spanner in the works was that Garrow and Lucy had formed a romantic attachment after Lucy had been ruled out as a suspect earlier in the investigation. Although they hadn't slept together, Garrow had been to Lucy's flat. As far as Garrow knew, there was no evidence that any of this had happened. What he didn't know was if Lucy's defence team was going to use this relationship to discredit him as the arresting officer and any evidence that he had gathered. And until they played their hand, he couldn't plan what he was going to say. He was also worried that Lucy would embellish and lie about what had really happened between them. Although Garrow had come clean to French about what he'd done, there was no point flagging it up to Ruth or his police federation rep until he knew what he was dealing with. The worrying thing was that Garrow could end up losing his job over it as he had effectively compromised a murder investigation. He could even face criminal prosecution himself.

He took a long deep breath to try and steady his nerves. His chest felt a little tight and his stomach was a ball of nerves. Taking out his phone, he could feel that his palms were sweaty. Even though the main corridor in the courthouse was stuffy, he knew it was anxiety that was making him sweat. He checked his messages and emails as a way of trying to distract himself. Then he sat back and tried to put the endless self-recrimination out of his head.

A teenage boy in a wheelchair was sitting opposite him on the other side of the wide corridor. He was with what looked like his elderly grandparents. They seemed to be consoling their grandson who looked incredibly upset. Garrow didn't know what 'their story' was or why they were there, but he got a sudden reminder of how self-absorbed and full of self-pity he was. He needed to remember that whatever happened today, it wasn't going to be the end of the world.

Looking up, he saw the barrister for the Crown Prosecution Service signal to him that the hearing was about to start in Court No 3.

Garrow got up, took a breath to steady himself again and walked down the corridor and into the courtroom. He took his seat a few rows behind where the defence team was sitting. He was due to give his testimony early on in the hearing.

A door opened on the far side of the courtroom and a figure appeared. It was Lucy Morgan. She was handcuffed to a female prison officer and led over to the area where defendants sat behind a perspex screen.

Garrow couldn't help but look in her direction. He was still kicking himself for being so naïve. He couldn't help it. Her hair was pulled back off her face and pinned back and she was wearing a smart business suit.

Suddenly Lucy turned and caught Garrow's eye. She gave him a friendly wink and then blew him a kiss.

Garrow looked away immediately as his heart sank. *This is not going to go well.*

Chapter 6

Half an hour later, Ruth and Nick were making their way towards Corwen where Major Leonard Nevin lived. As the only eyewitness, Ruth knew how important it was for them to talk to him as soon as possible. And given that he was in his 70s, she didn't want his memory of what he'd seen to fade.

On the journey, she had started to put in place what she needed for a murder investigation. The priority was to find any next of kin. The CID team at Llancastell was already trawling the electoral register and council tax records to see if they could establish if Aaron Jenkins was married or whether he lived with anyone.

Once the SOCOs had finished in the field, they needed to turn their attention to the farmhouse. Ruth wanted to find out as much as she could about Aaron Jenkins' life and why it had ended so violently. She was also concerned by the level of violence and the fact that he had been shot so many times.

Nick turned onto a narrow road and slowed down. The large detached houses to the right suggested this was an affluent area. Eventually they spotted *Holly Manor*, which was the address they'd been given for Major Nevin.

The house was Georgian in style with an immaculate sloping front garden that led up to stone steps and a large front door. The garden was bordered by box hedges and flower beds. Nearby was a swathe of apricot-coloured roses.

Knocking on the heavy oak door, Ruth took a step back and looked at Nick. *Holly Manor* was a far cry from the usual types of houses that they visited in their line of work. It had been a long time since they'd visited anywhere quite this grand. The warm summer air smelled of flowers and freshly cut grass.

The door was opened briskly and a well-dressed man in his 70s with a moustache peered out at them.

Ruth and Nick showed their warrant cards. 'DI Ruth Hunter and DS Nick Evans, Llancastell CID. We're looking for Major Leonard Nevin.'

'Yes, of course,' Leonard nodded in a plummy voice and opened the door wider. 'Please come in. And it's Leo. I haven't been a major for a long time.'

'Thank you,' Nick said as they went inside.

The hallway was large and spacious. The polished block wooden flooring was covered by a couple of dark red, patterned rugs. A looming grandfather clock stood at the foot of the stairs. An oval table with a cut glass vase filled with dried flowers was to their left. The air smelled of musty books and furniture polish.

'Please come through,' Leonard said as he ushered them into an enormous living room.

The walls had floor-to-ceiling bookshelves and there was a black, grand piano in the far corner that had a number of framed family photographs on top. Nearby there was a record player with various classical vinyl albums spread out on the table to its side – *Debussy*, *Elgar* and *Beethoven*.

Ruth and Nick sat down on a dark leather Chesterfield sofa as Leonard settled in an armchair opposite them.

Ruth noticed how uncomfortable the sofa was. Not only was it hard with virtually no give in it, the leather also made it quite slippy so it was difficult not to slide forward a little.

'Would you like some coffee or tea?' he asked them.

Ruth gave him a friendly smile and shook her head. 'We're fine thank you.'

'Bit of a shock seeing that today,' Leonard said as he crossed his legs. He was wearing dark brown corduroy trousers, Oxford brogues and colourful socks.

Ruth thought that he actually seemed remarkably calm for someone who had seen someone shot dead only two hours earlier.

'Yes, of course,' Nick said sympathetically as he pulled out his notepad and pen. 'Could you tell us exactly what you saw?'

'My wife and I had decided to take our grandchildren on the steam railway at Llangollen,' he explained. 'About two or three minutes after we had pulled out of the station, I just happened to see two men in a field that was adjacent to the railway line. And I saw that they were arguing. One of them pushed the other backwards.'

'Could you describe the people that you saw?' Ruth asked.

Leonard frowned. 'It was quite a distance. But the man with the gun was wearing a black hat and sunglasses.'

Nick raised an eyebrow. 'A hat?'

'Yes.' Leonard paused for a second. 'Sorry, it just happened so fast. It might have been one of those baseball caps.'

Ruth looked at him. 'And you're sure it was a man holding the gun?'

'Actually, now that you say that I couldn't swear to it.' Leonard pulled a face. 'I suppose it might have been a woman.'

'Could you see anything else? Was the person holding the gun tall or short? What was their build?'

'I'm sorry,' Leonard replied. 'If I had to guess, I suppose they were medium height and medium build. That's not very helpful.'

'That's fine. It's very helpful,' Ruth reassured him.

Nick stopped writing and glanced at him. 'Are you saying medium height and build for a man?' he asked to clarify.

Leonard nodded. 'Yes. I should have said that.'

'Did you see the other person?'

'Just for a second. The only thing I remember thinking is that he looked like a farmer and had a beard.'

Nick raised an eyebrow. 'Why did you think that?'

'I don't know.' Leonard shrugged. 'Just the clothes that he was wearing. I only saw him briefly.'

Ruth narrowed her eyes. 'But you did see the gun fire, is that correct?'

'Oh yes. I spent thirty five years in the British Army. I saw the muzzle flash. I'd know it anywhere. I was with 2 Para in the Falklands,' he explained. 'I was very young, but seeing that muzzle flash in the distance took me right back … I don't know why.'

Nick nodded. 'I don't suppose you happened to see the weapon that was fired?'

'Not exactly,' he said hesitantly.

Ruth gave him a curious look. 'Go on,' she prompted him.

'Well I can tell you it wasn't a handgun or a rifle. The

gun was fired from the hip. And there were several muzzle flashes all together. And that tells me that it was some kind of automatic weapon.'

'A machine gun?' Ruth asked, to clarify what he meant.

'Yes, exactly. Something relatively small. Technically you'd call it a submachine gun because of its size and the ammunition it uses.'

Nick furrowed his brow. 'Would it fire 9mm ammunition?'

'Yes.'

Ruth glanced at Nick. It sounded as if Aaron Jenkins had been shot and killed by some kind of automatic weapon, possibly his own. And that was very rare in this part of North Wales.

Chapter 7

It was 7am the following morning and Ruth was already on her second coffee. She sat back on her chair in the DI's office on the right hand side of the CID room. Looking out, she saw that most of the team were already in and working hard. The first 48 hours in a murder case were vital. Although their daily briefing was scheduled for 9am, Ruth wanted to get going and get everyone up to speed so she had pulled it forward to just after 7am. There was no time to waste.

Nick appeared at her open door with a printout. 'Aaron Jenkins was married to a Natalie. No kids. She's a primary school teacher in Llangollen. Her parents live up on the coast and she's been staying with them for the weekend. She's making her way back now and will be at Aaron's brother Charlie's house by 8am. He lives locally.'

'Okay, good,' Ruth said. 'We'll need to speak to her as soon as possible.'

'As far as I can see, no one else lives on the farm.'

Ruth glanced down at her watch. 'Right ... I'd better

get this briefing done. Then I think you and I need to go and see Natalie Jenkins.'

Getting up from her desk, Ruth picked up a file and her coffee and then wandered slowly out to the CID office.

'Right, listen up everyone,' she said in a raised voice as she strode purposefully towards the front of the office where a scene board had already been erected. At its centre was a photo of Aaron Jenkins that they'd found somewhere online, along with his date of birth, address, and apparent cause of death, etc. 'As most of you know, this is Aaron Jenkins, aged 41. He owns and runs Manor Farm just north of Llangollen. Yesterday afternoon an eyewitness saw him arguing with someone in the field that is adjacent to the Llangollen Heritage Railway. That person then brutally shot and killed Aaron. The description of that person is relatively vague. Possibly a black baseball cap, sunglasses, average height and build for a man. However, our eyewitness couldn't be sure if the person he saw was a man or a woman. Nick?'

Nick got up and went over to the scene board and pointed to a photograph. 'Officers found a gun cabinet that was empty except for this pack of 9mm ammunition.'

French looked confused. 'He had a handgun?'

'That was my first thought,' Nick replied. 'Our eyewitness, Leonard Nevin, is a retired army major. He is sure that the weapon he saw this person carrying and firing was a submachine gun. We have no way of knowing if that gun belonged to Aaron or our killer.'

'He wouldn't have a licence for that anyway, sarge,' Georgie pointed out.

'No,' Nick agreed, 'but let's run a check and see what firearms Aaron did have a licence for. We're waiting for the preliminary post-mortem but Ruth and I are sure that the gunshot wounds that Aaron received yesterday were not caused by a shotgun. So, that matches what our eyewitness saw.'

French looked puzzled. 'Doesn't make a lot of sense. A farmer being shot in his field by someone with a machine gun.'

'Not at first sight it doesn't,' Ruth agreed as she looked out at the team. 'I want us to get hold of Aaron's bank accounts and phone records. Search through his social media. I'd like to establish who the last person to see him was. I know that we've got initial statements from the properties adjacent to the farm but I'd like us to be more thorough. If our suspect was armed with an automatic firearm, this attack was planned and premeditated. And that means our suspect might well have been keeping an eye on Aaron and his farm in recent days or even weeks … Right, let's get going on this please everyone.'

Chapter 8

Garrow took a nervous gulp and looked around Mold Crown Court No 3 with trepidation. Even though it was the second day of a preliminary hearing, the public gallery was relatively full. And despite the searing temperature outside, the court was air conditioned and verging on chilly.

The defence barrister, Charles Bentley – 50s, tall, glasses and intense looking – glanced over at him with a frown. The questioning had been relatively straightforward so far, but Garrow knew that it was going to get trickier as they went on. He'd seen it before. A defence barrister lull a witness into a false sense of security before suddenly going on the attack and putting them 'on the ropes'.

'And you believed that the defendant, Lucy Morgan, was suffering from amnesia?' Bentley asked.

'Yes,' Garrow replied.

Bentley looked over from where he was sitting with the defence team. 'And there is no medical evidence to suggest that she wasn't suffering from a form of dissociative amnesia?'

'I'd like to raise a concern here,' the Crown Prosecution barrister interjected. 'DC Garrow is a police officer. He's not here to offer his opinion about medical evidence.'

The judge nodded. 'Yes, I agree.'

Bentley gave a supercilious smile at this. 'I'll rephrase the question then. Was it the opinion of you and your colleagues at Llancastell CID that Lucy Morgan was suffering from amnesia?'

Garrow nodded. 'Yes.'

Bentley got up from where he was sitting and took a few steps towards where Garrow was standing in the witness box. 'DC Garrow, could you describe your relationship with Lucy Morgan.'

Garrow's stomach tightened. *Here we go,* he thought.

'Relationship?' Garrow frowned. 'I don't have a relationship with the defendant.' As he said it, he could feel Lucy's glare across the court but he made sure that he didn't look in her direction or make eye contact. 'I was the investigating officer in the murder of her mother, Lynne Morgan.'

Bentley snorted and pulled a quizzical face. 'Really? You had no romantic relationship with Lucy Morgan during this investigation?'

'No,' Garrow said adamantly, even though it irked him to lie on the stand under oath.

'That's not true though, is it DC Garrow?' Bentley said in a patronising tone.

'We formed a bond,' Garrow admitted. He knew he couldn't deny that there had been something between them. It seemed prudent to say there had been a bond and that Lucy had now embellished that to discredit him as a police officer.

'A bond?' Bentley scoffed. 'Define 'bond' for us would you please?'

'With any crime like this, where an officer gets to know the family of a victim, there is a natural bond,' Garrow explained, treading very carefully. 'It's a very emotional time for everyone.'

'And would you say that you form this type of bond in every investigation of this nature?' Bentley asked.

The Crown Prosecution barrister looked at the judge. 'Can I ask where my learned friend is going with this line of questioning?'

The judge nodded in agreement. 'If you could get to the point you're trying to make a little quicker please.'

'DC Garrow, when you form a bond with someone you meet during an investigation, would you normally kiss or have sexual relations with that person?' Bentley enquired.

Garrow felt his pulse begin to race.

'No, of course not,' he replied, trying to remain as calm as he could. Now he knew that Lucy was going to claim that they'd had a sexual relationship even though that was a lie. They hadn't even kissed, for God's sake.

'Really?' Bentley asked derisively. 'You didn't have sex with the defendant?'

'No, I did not,' Garrow replied slowly.

'But you've been to her flat, haven't you?'

Garrow nodded. 'Myself and DS French went to Lucy Morgan's flat when we believed she was suffering from amnesia to see if there was anything we could discover that might help her regain her memory.'

'Oh, right,' Bentley said, nodding his head slowly. 'And that was the only time you visited her flat was it?'

'As far as I recall, yes,' he replied, but he was getting nervous about what was coming next.

'Really?' Bentley went over to his notes for a moment and then turned around. 'DC Garrow, you went to Lucy

Morgan's flat on Friday 9th April where you shared a glass of wine and then had sex, didn't you?'

'No,' Garrow replied, aware that his voice was at a slightly higher pitch than before. 'That didn't happen.'

'You didn't go into Lucy Morgan's flat on that date?' Bentley asked forcefully.

Garrow took a moment to reply. If he lied and said that he didn't, that would open him up to an accusation of lying if there was an eyewitness who had seen him go in. But if no one had seen him going in, it was just Lucy's word against his. Like some nerve-racking game of poker, Garrow had no idea what the other side were holding 'in their hand'.

Play safe, he told himself.

'Yes, I did,' he said quietly.

'Sorry?' Bentley asked, clearly pretending that he hadn't heard Garrow's answer.

'Yes, I did go into her flat,' he repeated.

'So you did have sex with Lucy Morgan on that date?' he stated.

Garrow shook his head. 'No. I didn't.'

Bentley stared at him. 'But you did have a glass of wine?'

Garrow took another moment. Lucy had poured him a glass of wine just before he'd arrested her for her mother's murder. And when forensics officers went to the flat, they would have found two empty glasses. If the defence had access to that information, they could prove he was lying.

'Yes, I did have a glass of wine,' he admitted.

'DC Garrow,' Bentley said. 'Do you make a habit of going alone to the homes of the women you meet during investigations and drinking wine with them?'

Garrow shook his head. 'No, I don't.'

'But you did this time. And then you had sex with Lucy Morgan, didn't you?' Bentley snapped.

'No.'

Bentley snorted and shook his head. 'You want us to believe that you lied to us about going with Lucy into her flat on the 9th April. And that you lied about having a glass of wine. But you have told us the truth about not having sex with the defendant, is that right?'

'Yes.'

Bentley gave a pompous smile. 'You seem very confused, DC Garrow. Maybe you should have got your fanciful story straight in your mind before you came to the witness box.'

Chapter 9

Ruth and Nick pulled up outside the address in Llangollen they'd been given for Aaron Jenkins' brother, Charlie. It was a cul-de-sac with lots of small, neat new-build homes. Half a dozen children were out on the road on bikes or playing in the late afternoon sunshine.

Looking up, Ruth could see the ruins of Castell Dinas Bran high on a hilltop in the distance. Built in the 13th century, the remnants of the old medieval castle were over 1,000ft above sea level, making it the highest castle in Wales or England. There had been much debate over what Dinas Bran could be translated as. It had been traditionally called 'crow's fortress', although the anglicised 'crow castle' was also popular.

Ruth popped on her sunglasses as she got out of the car and closed the passenger door. She would wait until they had spoken to Aaron Jenkins' widow before having her next cigarette.

The house looked relatively new, and a white Audi A5 was parked on the gravel drive. Ruth went to the front door which had frosted glass and knocked. Then she and

Nick took out their warrant cards, although she was expecting to see the family liaison officer – FLO – who had been assigned to Natalie now that this was a murder case.

The front door opened and a tall, young uniformed officer with a goatee beard looked out at them.

'DI Hunter and DS Evans, Llancastell CID,' Ruth explained. 'We've come to speak to Natalie Jenkins.'

The officer nodded calmly. 'Of course, ma'am,' he said as he opened the door fully to allow them inside.

The hallway was neat, with a row of hooks containing raincoats and jackets that clearly belonged to young children. The house smelled of toast and coffee.

'Natalie is through here,' he said as he went to a closed door to their left.

Ruth's phone rang. It was the CID office. She signalled to the officer to give them a second before opening the door.

'DI Hunter?' she said, answering the phone.

'Boss, it's Georgie. Intel has come through about Manor Farm. According to HMRC records, Aaron Jenkins had started the process of filing for bankruptcy about two months ago.'

That's interesting, Ruth thought immediately.

'Do we know why?' she asked.

'Mortgage arrears, unpaid bills,' Georgie explained. 'I need to look at the bank records to see if there are any anomalies.'

'Okay, keep me posted. Good work, Georgie.'

Ending the call, Ruth then looked at the officer and gestured to the door.

'We'll go in now,' she said.

'Yes, ma'am,' he replied. Even after all these years, being called *ma'am* still grated on Ruth.

'We'll take it from here,' she reassured him as she opened the door and she and Nick went into a living room.

A woman in her late 30s, whom she assumed was Natalie Jenkins, was sitting clutching a tissue and looking vacantly out of the window. A stocky man in his 40s sat in a nearby armchair. Ruth assumed this was Aaron's brother Charlie.

'Hi there,' Ruth said gently as they came in. 'I'm DI Ruth Hunter and this is DS Nick Evans. We're from CID in Llancastell. I'm so sorry for your loss.' Ruth gestured to the sofa. 'Mind if we sit down?'

Natalie looked confused for a moment as if she hadn't heard what Ruth had asked.

'Of course,' the man said with a very serious expression. 'I'm Charlie … I'm Aaron's brother.'

Nick nodded as they sat down. 'Thank you.'

Ruth leaned forward and gave Natalie an empathetic look. She had mousy hair tied back, no makeup and wore a navy sweater and jeans. She had that vacant look that Ruth had seen so many times in her line of work. Grief, disbelief, denial and pain.

'I know this is a very difficult time for you, Natalie,' she said quietly, 'but we'd like to ask you some questions.'

'Is that really necessary?' Charlie asked.

Natalie gave him a look. 'It's fine, Charlie. Really.' Ruth noticed that she didn't have a Welsh accent. In fact she sounded as if she had a slightly Liverpudlian twang.

Nick pulled out his notebook and pen. 'You've been away this weekend, is that correct?'

Natalie nodded. 'Yes. I was visiting my parents.'

'And where do they live?' he asked.

'Llandudno. They retired and moved over there a few years ago.'

Ruth frowned. 'But Aaron didn't go with you?'

Natalie shared a look with Charlie which Ruth spotted.

'Aaron didn't really get on with my parents,' she explained.

'Can I ask why?'

'They're snobs,' Charlie said caustically.

Natalie shook her head. 'They're not snobs. I think they had very set ideas of the sort of man they wanted me to marry.'

'Yeah, not a Welsh farmer,' Charlie snorted with more than a hint of bitterness.

Nick looked at her. 'How long had you and Aaron been married?'

'Eight years. Nearly nine.' The question seemed to have upset her. She took a deep breath and wiped a tear from her eye. 'Sorry.'

Ruth shook her head. 'You don't need to apologise.'

'And you don't have children, is that right?' Nick asked delicately.

'Yeah … I mean no, we don't.'

'How did Aaron seem recently? Was there anything bothering him?' Ruth enquired.

Natalie looked over at Charlie who shook his head.

'No. Nothing I can think of,' she said.

'No. Aaron seemed his usual self, didn't he?' Charlie agreed, looking at Natalie.

'Yes.'

Maybe it was her imagination but Ruth picked up on something between Natalie and Charlie. A slight nervousness as if they were hiding something from them. And also a closeness that felt unusual for a woman and her brother-in-law.

Nick glanced over. 'Can you think of anyone who might have wanted to harm your husband? Any recent arguments with anyone?'

Natalie narrowed her eyes. 'No. Aaron wasn't like that. Apart from going to the pub to play darts, he kept himself to himself.'

'Which pub is that?'

'The Red Lion,' she replied.

'And you didn't have any financial problems concerning the farm or anything like that?' Ruth asked, as a way of finding out what Natalie actually knew.

'No. I don't think so.' Natalie shook her head innocently. 'Aaron deals with all that sort of thing, but as far as I'm aware there wasn't a problem.'

'And you're a teacher, is that right?' Nick said.

'Yes. St Mary's, just up the road.'

Ruth looked directly at her. 'So you had no idea that Aaron had started to file for bankruptcy in recent weeks?'

Natalie took a few seconds to process what Ruth had said.

'What?' Her eyes widened in shock. Then she shook her head. 'No. That can't be right. Aaron would have said something.'

'That can't be right,' Charlie protested, and then looked directly at Natalie. 'He knew he could come to me with something like that.'

As far as Ruth could see, neither Natalie or Charlie had any idea about the financial difficulties that the farm was in.

Ruth raised an eyebrow. 'I'm afraid that Aaron had been to see a solicitor to begin the process.'

Natalie looked over at Charlie with tears in her eyes. 'Why didn't he say something?'

Charlie frowned. 'I don't understand,' he said with a bewildered expression.

Nick sat forward. 'Do you know what Aaron's movements were yesterday?'

Natalie nodded, sniffed and wiped her face with a tissue. 'Yeah. He texted me around eleven. He said that he was going to The Red Lion for a pint and to play darts. That was the last thing I heard.'

Ruth knew that the eyewitness had seen Aaron being shot at around 2pm which was three hours later.

'There are just a couple more things and then we can get going,' Ruth said gently. 'We haven't managed to find a mobile phone. Did Aaron have a phone?'

'Yes,' Natalie replied.

'If you could give us his number, that would save us a lot of time,' Nick explained.

'Of course,' Charlie said as he reached into his pocket, tapped on his iPhone and then read out Aaron's mobile number which Nick scribbled down.

'Thank you,' Nick said as he shifted in his seat. 'We noticed that you have a locked gun cabinet in the farmhouse.'

At this stage, it was prudent not to let on what they'd found in there and allow Natalie to tell them what she knew – or at least, what she was willing to tell them.

Aaron has a couple of shotguns in there,' she explained. She looked confused by the question. 'Was he shot with one of his own guns?'

Ruth shook her head. 'No. The gun that killed Aaron wasn't a shotgun,' she said gently.

'Do you have a key to that gun cabinet?' Nick asked.

'If Aaron wasn't shot by a shotgun, why are you so interested in his gun cabinet?' Charlie asked, sounding irritable.

Ruth met Natalie's gaze. 'If you could answer the question please, Natalie.'

'Oh yes,' she said, sounding distracted. Ruth couldn't

work out if the questions about the guns had rattled her slightly. 'Erm, no. Aaron had the keys to the cabinet.'

'Where did he keep them?' Nick asked.

'I don't know. I've never even fired a gun,' Natalie said, but there was something unconvincing in her answer.

Ruth narrowed her eyes. 'And do you know exactly what he kept in there?'

Natalie shrugged. 'He just had a couple of shotguns, that's all.' Then she gave Charlie a fleeting glance which he ignored.

Something was definitely up.

Nick furrowed his brow. 'Would it surprise you if we told you that when officers arrived at your farmhouse, they found the gun cabinet open. It was empty, except for a box of 9mm ammunition.'

Natalie took a moment as her eyes roamed around the room. 'I don't even know what that is.'

'9mm?' Charlie asked. 'That doesn't make any sense.'

'What does it mean?' Natalie asked them.

Charlie looked at her. 'You'd use 9mm ammo for a handgun or an automatic weapon.'

He's very knowledgeable.

Ruth raised an eyebrow. 'You seem to know your stuff?'

'I was in the army,' he explained. 'So were both my brothers.'

'You have another brother?' Nick asked.

'Had,' Charlie corrected him. 'Our elder brother Lee was shot and killed in Afghanistan in 2007. I don't think Aaron ever really got over it.'

Chapter 10

It was early evening as Ruth and Nick headed back out of Llangollen towards The Red Lion pub. The sky above them was still a beautiful azure blue with a series of long, thin, wispy white clouds that looked like pulled cotton wool. Ruth watched for a moment as the sunlight dappled across the windscreen through the branches of the trees that loomed over the road. In any other circumstances it would have been a perfect evening.

Then Ruth took a cigarette from the packet, tapped it and popped it in her mouth. She buzzed down the window and grabbed her lighter.

'Ex-army? That has to be significant, doesn't it?' Nick said, thinking out loud.

Ruth nodded as she lit her cigarette, took a deep drag, blew it out of the open window and watched as the wind snatched it away.

'Aaron Jenkins was shot by an automatic weapon. We found 9mm ammunition in his gun cabinet,' Ruth replied thoughtfully. 'It seems to be too much of a coincidence that he's ex-military for it not to be connected.'

'What did you think of his brother?'

As they rounded the corner of a long bend, The Red Lion pub appeared on the left-hand side. It was set back from the road with a large car park to one side.

'I wasn't sure. He seemed guarded,' Ruth conceded. 'They were both hiding something from us.'

Nick nodded as he indicated to turn left into the pub car park.

'They were very twitchy about the gun cabinet and the guns,' he stated.

He pulled into the car park and headed for a space close to the entrance.

Then he glanced at Ruth and raised an eyebrow quizzically. 'You think there's something going on there?'

'I'm not sure,' she said, 'but it's definitely something we should have a closer look at.'

As they got out of the car, Ruth took another drag on her cigarette before putting it out on the metallic stubbing plate on top of a nearby bin. The air was like a warm blanket as she and Nick turned and headed for the double doors that led into the pub.

The inside of The Red Lion had clearly been recently renovated. It was now painted in subtle shades of light greens, with wooden furniture and several blackboards displaying an extensive wine list and menu.

They approached the bar where a young man in his mid-20s was standing. He had jet black hair, beard, olive skin and looked like he might be Mediterranean. He was taking off a leather jacket and held a black motorcycle helmet under his arm. He had clearly just arrived for work.

The man hung up his jacket, put the helmet to one side and then turned to face them. 'Hi there,' he said in a friendly voice that had a distinct accent. 'What can I get you?'

'Hi. We're DI Hunter and DS Evans,' Ruth said as they showed him their warrant cards. 'Llangollen CID. Is the manager around?'

The man shook his head. 'I'm afraid not. Can I help?' he replied very politely.

Ruth looked at him. 'Sorry, we didn't get your name?'

'Haji.'

'Haji,' Ruth repeated.

'It's Moroccan,' he explained.

Nick moved closer to the bar so that they could talk quietly. 'Do you know an Aaron Jenkins?'

Haji nodded immediately. 'Yes. He's a regular in here.'

'Did you see him in here yesterday?' Ruth enquired.

He shook his head. 'No, sorry. Yesterday was my day off, so I wasn't here.' Then he gestured to a young woman in her late 20s who was clearing away some plates from a nearby table. 'Bethan was working though.'

Bethan had fashionable dyed blonde and blue hair, nose and eyebrow piercings, and was attractive. As she came over to the bar, she gave Ruth and Nick a quizzical look.

'They're police officers,' Haji said by way of an explanation. 'They wanted to know if Aaron was in here yesterday.'

Bethan gave them a defensive scowl. 'Aaron?' she asked in a thick North Wales accent. 'Yeah, he was. Why?'

She seems a bit shifty and wary, Ruth thought to herself.

Nick gave Bethan a forced smile. 'Could you tell us exactly what time he was here?'

'Why? What's he done?' she asked with a hostile frown.

Ruth waited for a second and then said very quietly, 'I'm afraid we have some very bad news. Aaron was murdered yesterday afternoon, so we're going to need you to cooperate with us in our investigation.'

The blood drained from Bethan's face. 'What?' she gasped.

'Oh God, that's terrible,' Haji muttered.

'Murdered?' Bethan whispered as she shook her head. Then her eyes filled with tears. 'I don't understand.' She seemed completely overwhelmed by the news. Whatever her and Aaron's relationship was, it was clear that they had been close.

'Could you tell us what time he was in here yesterday?' Nick asked quietly.

'Erm, yeah. Of course.' Bethan was a bit shaky as she bit her lip. 'It was early. Eleven thirty.'

'Was he with anyone?' Ruth asked.

'He didn't come in with anyone,' Bethan said, but it was clear there was more to her answer.

Nick looked at her. 'Did you speak to him?'

'Yeah.' Bethan nodded but the news had knocked her for six. 'He ordered a drink.'

'How did he seem?'

Bethan shrugged. 'Fine. He was fine.'

'Did he speak to anyone or meet anyone?' Ruth asked.

Bethan nodded but didn't say anything. Then she wiped the tears from her face.

After a few seconds, she pointed to a small table in the far corner. 'He sat over there. And then a man came in and sat down with him.'

Ruth nodded encouragingly and asked, 'Could you describe the man for us, Bethan?'

Bethan thought for a moment. 'He was about the same age. Forty. He had a shaved head. Quite tall, I think.'

'Had you ever seen him before?'

'No.'

'And how long did they talk for?' Nick said.

'About half an hour.'

'And how did they seem?' Ruth asked.

Bethan seemed confused by the question.

'Were they laughing and joking?'

Bethan shook her head immediately. 'It seemed that they were talking about something serious. And they were talking quietly as if they didn't want anyone to hear what they were saying.'

'Did this man buy a drink?' Nick enquired.

'Yes. He bought two pints of lager.'

'Did he pay with cash or card?'

If he'd used a card then there might be a way of tracing him.

'Cash.'

Shame.

'Did he have an accent?'

Bethan shrugged. 'Sounded like he came from around here.'

'He had a North Wales accent?' Ruth asked to clarify.

'Yeah.'

Nick rubbed his jawline and asked, 'Did the man leave before or after Aaron?'

'They left together.'

Ruth had a thought as she looked around the pub's interior. 'Have you got CCTV in here or outside?'

Bethan seemed overwhelmed by the news of Aaron's death. She was lost somewhere in her own thoughts.

'Bethan?' Ruth said softly.

'Sorry,' she mumbled. 'Erm, we've got a camera out in the car park.'

Ruth and Nick shared a look.

'We're going to need to have a look,' Ruth told her gently.

Bethan pointed to Haji. 'I don't really know how to

work it. But Haji does.' She gave him a signal to come down the bar to where they were standing.

'Haji,' Ruth said. 'Bethan says that you can show us the car park CCTV from yesterday morning?'

He gave a helpful nod. 'Yes, of course.' Then he pointed to a door behind the bar down on their left. 'The computer is in there if you want me to show you?'

'Thank you,' Nick said with a half-smile as they followed him behind the bar.

Ruth noticed that the smell of stale beer and alcohol was much stronger now they were on the other side of the bar. As a recovering alcoholic, Ruth wondered how Nick felt being surrounded by booze.

Haji opened the door and showed them into a small office. On the far wall there were shelves that were lined with box files and accounts. There was a small black sofa, chair and coffee table to their left. On the right, there was a desk with a PC and monitor.

Grabbing the office chair, Haji opened up the computer, went onto the desktop and clicked CCTV. Inside were a series of MP4 files with dates.

'Here we go,' he said as he clicked the mouse and the CCTV of the car park appeared on the screen.

'And this is from yesterday?' Ruth asked to clarify.

Haji nodded.

'Great,' Nick said. 'If we can play it from 11.30am.'

Haji rewound the file until the timecode at the bottom of the screen read *11.30 am*. Then he played it forward at x2 speed.

Almost immediately, a red Toyota pickup truck drove into the car park.

A figure got out.

It was Aaron Jenkins.

He headed into the pub.

As the timecode reached *11.56am*, a white BMW X5 pulled into the car park.

A man got out.

He was tall, early 40s, wearing a black baseball cap and sunglasses.

'Can you stop it there?' Ruth asked.

Haji paused the CCTV.

'That's got to be our man,' Ruth said, peering at the screen. However, there was very little to go on as the baseball cap and sunglasses hid his features.

Nick scribbled in his notebook. 'And we've got his registration.'

Ruth pointed to the screen. 'Can we play it forward to when they leave?'

'Of course.' Haji played the footage forward to *12.53pm.*

Two figures came into view as they left the pub together.

It was Aaron and the man they'd seen arriving in the BMW.

'Can you stop it just there, please?' Ruth said as she went closer to the screen.

The man from the BMW had a logo of some kind on the back of his navy t-shirt.

'PTC Security,' Ruth said, reading out the words on the logo for Nick to write down.

They then watched as the two men went back to their vehicles and drove away.

They had no idea if this was the man who had been seen from the train shooting Aaron Jenkins.

But what they did know was that within two hours of leaving the pub, Aaron had been murdered.

Chapter 11

It was 10pm by the time Ruth eventually got home. Her plan was to have a large glass of wine, food, shower, four to five hours' sleep and then go back into CID. That's just how it was when there was a major incident such as a murder. She would be able to take some time in lieu when things calmed down again.

Gazing up into the sky, Ruth sat out on the patio with the warm night breeze soft against her face. A half-moon had now appeared, and in the distance the horizon was showing the faintest touches of indigo as the light of the day was finally extinguished.

Taking out her phone, she remembered that she needed to call Garrow to check how things were going in court. She could really do with him back in CID as they were now a DC down without him.

'Hi boss,' he said as he answered her call.

'Sorry for the late call, Jim,' Ruth apologised. 'I just wanted to check in. How did it go yesterday and today?'

There was an awkward silence. She assumed from this that things weren't going well.

'If I'm honest, I don't think they could have gone any worse,' Garrow said very quietly. He sounded rattled.

Ruth wondered what he meant and why it had gone so wrong. 'What happened?'

'Lucy Morgan is accusing me of having sex with her before she was arrested.'

'But you didn't.'

'No,' Garrow said.

However, Ruth sensed there was a 'but' coming. As far as she knew, Garrow and Lucy Morgan had struck up no more than the beginnings of a friendship.

'I've got a horrible feeling that there's something you haven't told me,' she said quietly.

She heard Garrow take a breath. *This isn't good,* she thought.

'Just before I got the news from Dan that a knife had been found hidden at Pontcysyllte Aqueduct,' Garrow explained, 'I'd gone into Lucy Morgan's flat and had a glass of wine with her.'

'Jesus Christ, Jim!' Ruth couldn't hide her annoyance.

'Nothing happened, boss,' he said meekly, 'I promise you. Dan called me and I arrested her there and then.'

Ruth sighed. 'But you made yourself incredibly vulnerable by doing that, didn't you?'

'Yes. It was idiotic,' he admitted.

'And now I'm guessing that the defence are trying to say that all your evidence is inadmissible at trial?'

'Yes.'

'And if that's the case, there won't be a trial,' Ruth groaned. 'What a bloody mess, Jim.'

'I'm sorry for not protecting myself,' he said, 'and I'm sorry for lying to you, boss.'

'Look, let's see how things pan out at court tomorrow,' Ruth said, now trying to reassure Garrow. He was a young officer who knew he'd made a big mistake. Tearing a strip off him wasn't going to help matters.

'Okay. Thanks for checking in,' he said, and ended the call.

Sarah appeared with two large glasses of rosé. 'Here we go.'

'You're an angel,' Ruth said as she reached out to take one.

'I know.' Sarah laughed as she sat down. 'And I have some good news.'

Ruth sighed. 'Well I definitely need some good news after today. I was looking forward to a lovely barbeque this afternoon. Instead I had to try to identify a man who had been shot to pieces in a field.'

'Perks of the job,' Sarah joked darkly. Then she looked over. 'The adoption people are coming over in two weeks' time with Susannah. She seems to think that if they can sign off on us, then the adoption is as good as approved.'

Ruth smiled and took a long swig of wine. 'That's fantastic news.'

Chapter 12

It was 5.30am as Ruth entered the CID office at Llancastell nick. There were a couple of detectives from the night shift working at computers. They'd be there until about 9am and then go home. However, now that they had a murder to investigate, shift patterns often just went out of the window. It was all hands on deck, and often shifts just merged into each other. The only issue came when certain detectives – usually male – tried to prove their resilience by working 24 hours on the bounce. Ruth actively discouraged this. Tired detectives made mistakes. It only took an exhausted officer to overlook a tiny detail and the investigation could be set back significantly.

Walking into her office, Ruth got the lovely smell of polish and the 'freshly vacuumed' odour. She had just missed the cleaners who were normally finished in CID by around 5am. Up on her wall was a blue poster with a new nationwide police initiative – *Project Servator* – written in big white letters. It had started around ten years ago as a counter-terrorism scheme, but now it encompassed any operations that aimed to disrupt organised criminals.

Sitting down on her office chair, Ruth stretched out her back and spine. She was pretty certain that she was getting stiffer and less supple with every month that went past. Sarah had suggested that they go to a weekly yoga class, which Ruth thought was a good idea. It was just finding the time.

A figure approached. It was Nick. He was holding a printout.

He glanced at his watch and grinned. 'What time do you call this?'

Ruth frowned. 'What time did you get in?'

'Five on the dot,' he replied with a mocking shrug.

Ruth raised an eyebrow. 'What for?'

Nick hesitated. 'Megan keeps waking up so …'

'So you do a runner into work before she does?' Ruth said, shaking her head.

'Sort of,' he admitted. 'And we do have a murder case, boss.'

'Yeah. Pull the other one, it's got bells on it,' she joked. 'What's that?'

'Aaron Jenkins' military record. Welsh Guards regiment. Did ten years and reached the rank of Corporal. Two tours of Afghanistan in 2007 and 2009. And as we know, his older brother, Lee, was killed there in July 2007.'

'All three brothers were in the Welsh Guards?'

Nick nodded. 'Yes. Charles, or Charlie, Jenkins left the regiment in 2019. He's the youngest brother.'

Ruth arched her brows. 'Did Aaron buy Manor Farm when he left the army then?'

Nick shook his head. 'Land Registery records show that he inherited it from his father, Dewi, in 2017.'

'What about Charlie?'

'I haven't got details of the will,' Nick admitted.

'But we do know that Manor Farm was about to go bankrupt,' Ruth said, thinking out loud.

'Maybe that was a source of conflict between the brothers,' Nick suggested.

'And if there's anything going on between Charlie and Natalie,' Ruth said, 'we've got a decent amount of motive.'

Nick looked doubtful. 'Except we know that the man that Aaron met in the pub on Monday morning wasn't his brother.'

'True, but my instinct is for us to look at the brother and wife before we look anywhere else.'

'Right you are,' Nick said as he turned to go.

Ruth knew that 90% of UK homicides were committed by a family member or person known to the victim. That meant they needed to take a very close look at Charlie and Natalie Jenkins.

Chapter 13

It was 9am and Garrow had been summoned into the Crown Prosecution Service office within Mold Crown Court for what was due to be the third day of the preliminary hearing. The office was dark and old-fashioned. The walls were lined with floor-to-ceiling shelves that were filled with bound legal cases and books. The dark, wood furniture looked like it had been there for decades, and the air was musty like that of an old library.

The chief barrister for the CPS, Adrian Holloway, sat behind a large oak desk with a PC to one side. In his late 50s, Holloway had a smattering of blond hair on the sides of his bald head, piercing blue eyes, glasses and a pointed nose and chin. He looked incredibly serious.

Garrow was feeling anxious after the events of the previous day. He knew that his performance on the witness stand when questioned by the defence barrister had been verging on disastrous. The barrister had probably done enough to cast doubt on all of Garrow's testimony. It didn't matter that it was Garrow's word against Lucy Morgan's. He had admitted going into the suspect's flat while off duty and having a glass of wine. Lucy's claims that they had had sex allowed the defence team to paint a picture of Garrow as a completely unreliable witness. And if that was true, then the whole case for the prosecution was compromised.

Garrow was kicking himself for being so naïve. How had he allowed himself to get close to someone like Lucy? It confirmed all the dark misgivings that he had about himself as a police officer. That he wasn't streetwise or tough enough to make it as a detective. However astute and cerebral Garrow was in his approach to police work, he worried that he lacked the more intuitive aspects of detection. Moreover, the whole thing played into his fear that he was gullible when it came to women.

Garrow had had his heart broken at university, and since then he'd struggled to form another romantic relationship of any note. In his second year at university, he had met and fallen in love with Lizzie. She was a post-graduate student, doing a master's in philosophy. She was bright and beautiful. Garrow loved everything about her. They would often sit in her tiny flat, drinking red wine and talking into the early hours. They seemed to share the same views on politics, theatre, film and literature. Garrow had never felt so energised and enthralled by someone. Lizzie's family were all intellectuals. Her father was a professor of economics at Christ's College, Cambridge. Her mother was a headteacher, and her brother the CEO of a charity. It was such a different world to the one he'd grown up in. Lizzie had the kind of family that Garrow wished he'd had. He knew that was unfair and churlish after all that his parents had given him. But he yearned for more stimulating conversations at home than local tittle-tattle, football and moronic, knee-jerk, right-wing politics. Garrow remembered going by train to Cambridge with Lizzie. Her father, Edward, had shown him around the various Cambridge colleges. They'd met Lizzie's mother for lunch at The Mill, an iconic 19th century pub that was located on the grassy banks of the River Cam where students went punting on hot summer days. And Garrow's imagination ran away with him. He pictured a life with Lizzie and all that went with that. He was overwhelmed by joy and excitement at their future together.

However, ever since they'd started seeing each other, Garrow had found Lizzie's tendency to blow hot and cold very undermining. They would spend a wonderful weekend together making love, cooking, listening to music and talking. And then Lizzie would tell him that she was busy for the next ten days or two weeks so she didn't have time to see him. As a one-off, that would have been fine. But as a continual pattern of behaviour, it left Garrow floundering. He knew that what he should have said was that if Lizzie didn't want to be in a proper relationship with him then it wouldn't work. But he didn't want to give up the fantasy of their future life that he'd built in his head. So he clung on.

Then one day, quite by chance, he spotted Lizzie coming out of a pub hand in hand with one of the university professors. He remembered feeling physically sick at what he'd seen. Rather than running after her to confront her, he sloped back home and got drunk. When he did finally turn up on her doorstep demanding an explanation, Lizzie admitted that she'd been sleeping with her professor for several months. She told Garrow that he was sweet, but too needy. And that was that. It felt like his whole world had collapsed in on him. He was devastated. And until he'd met Lucy Morgan, he had kept any women that he'd met at arms length in an effort to protect himself.

'The counsel for the defence has told us to drop the

charges against Lucy Morgan,' Holloway said, breaking Garrow's train of thought.

'What?' Garrow said, shaking his head, even though this is what he'd feared was going to happen.

'You can't be surprised,' Holloway snapped. 'Your testimony was a fucking shit show, Detective Constable Garrow. What the hell were you thinking?'

Silence.

Garrow took a moment. If the CPS did in fact drop the charges, that information would filter back to the senior ranking officers at Llancastell nick. He could find himself suspended or even out of a job.

'I just didn't think that Lucy Morgan could have murdered her mother,' Garrow admitted. 'She was so incredibly convincing.'

Holloway rolled his eyes. 'If you're going to be that naïve, then maybe you should reconsider your future as a police officer.'

Chapter 14

Ruth had been running the morning briefing with the CID team at Llancastell nick for about fifteen minutes. She had brought everyone up to speed with what they knew so far. She could feel a sense of urgency as she knew how important the first 48 hours were in a major incident like this.

'Have we had any luck tracing Aaron's phone yet?' she asked.

French looked over. 'Digital forensics have managed to triangulate the signal, boss. They're convinced that it's somewhere inside his farmhouse.'

Ruth gave French a dubious look. That didn't make any sense. 'But we've had the SOCOs in there.' It was rare for the forensic officers to miss something as important as the victim's phone.

French shrugged. 'That's what the GPS is telling them.'

'Anything on bank records and his phone records?'

'Arriving this morning, boss,' Georgie replied. 'I've trawled through Aaron's social media but there's nothing obvious there. Most of the groups that he's in on Facebook are ex-military. Welsh Guards regiment and veterans of the war in Afghanistan.'

Ruth perched herself on the edge of a table. 'Anything on that BMW registration from The Red Lion car park CCTV?'

DC Jade Kennedy sat forward in her seat. She had taken some time off while she moved home from Chester to North Wales. However, Ruth had contacted her to say that she needed her in, especially as DC Garrow was at court. 'I've just spoken to the DVLA. The car is registered to a PTC Security.'

'Thank you, Jade,' Ruth said, 'and I appreciate you being here this morning.'

'No problem, boss,' she replied.

Nick narrowed his eyes. 'Any idea who they are or where they're based?'

'As far as I can see, they're a recruitment company that finds security jobs for ex-military,' Kennedy explained. 'According to Companies House, the company is based in Corwen.'

Ruth nodded. 'If the farm was going bankrupt, then maybe Aaron was looking for a job elsewhere.'

Nick's phone rang. He answered it and moved away for a moment.

Ruth looked at Kennedy. 'Jade, you and Dan go and have a chat with the people at PTC and see if you can find out who met with Aaron on Monday and why.'

'Yes, boss.'

Nick looked over and gestured to his phone. 'The preliminary post-mortem has been done and Professor Amis would like us to go over for a chat.'

Ruth pulled a face. 'Oh great.' She found Amis frustratingly obtuse at the best of times.

She threw Nick the car keys. 'Come on then. You drive, I'll smoke.'

Chapter 15

Ruth pushed through the double doors into the Llancastell University Hospital mortuary, followed by Nick. The air with thick with the smell of preserving chemicals and detergents, and the temperature dropped to a ghostly chill. When she had been working as a DC in South London, she had attended many post-mortems – usually at King's College Hospital in Denmark Hill, Camberwell. Until the old Victorian hospital had been revamped in 2000 with a new 'Golden Jubilee Wing', King's had felt archaic. However, it struck Ruth as she looked around at the mortuary examination tables, gurneys, aluminium trays, workbenches, and an assortment of luminous chemicals, that this was one element of .police work that hadn't changed drastically in the past few decades.

Looking around, she spotted the Chief Pathologist, Professor Tony Amis. He was on the far side of the mortuary taking photographs, using a small white plastic ruler to give an indication of scale. Attached to his scrubs was a small microphone, as post-mortems were all now digitally recorded.

As Amis moved away from the metallic gurney, Ruth saw the pale, naked corpse of Aaron Jenkins laid out. Now that all the forensic evidence had been taken from him, Amis was establishing the cause of death, plus anything else that might help the investigation.

As Ruth approached, her gaze fixed on Aaron's lifeless body. There were five dark bullet holes – two in his abdomen, one in the middle of his chest and two in his legs.

'Rare to see wounds from an automatic weapon around here,' Amis commented as he gestured to Aaron. 'It's usually shotgun wounds.'

The front of Aaron's torso had a large scar where he had been cut open for examination. It had been stitched back up with blue thread.

'What can you tell us?' Ruth asked as they approached.

AMIS PULLED up his mask to reveal his patchy, ginger beard. Then he reached for a mug of tea on a nearby table. The mug had yet another witty statement printed on it. There was the red line of a heart monitor – *Handsome enough to stop your heart. Skilled enough to restart it again.*

Ruth chortled to herself. It was one of his better humorous mugs.

'Cause of death?'

'Your victim died from gunshot wounds,' Amis said casually as he slurped his tea. 'It was the one through the chest that did the real damage. Clipped his heart as it went through, which caused massive haemorrhaging. He would have been dead in less than thirty seconds.'

'Did you manage to retrieve any of the bullets?'

Amis nodded. 'We got a couple. The others went straight through him so they could be anywhere.' He then went to a small metallic dish and showed them. Inside were two flattened steel bullets. 'This one hit his ribs, ricocheted around and then lodged in his left lung.'

Nick raised an eyebrow. 'Any idea of calibre yet?'

Amis thought for a moment. 'If I had to guess from its size I'd say 9mm, but it will need to be checked.'

Why are we here? Ruth wondered. Amis could have told them that over the phone and saved them a journey across town.

'But I wanted you to see this,' he said as he put down his mug and flicked on a spotlight. He dragged it over so that it shone brightly on the back of Aaron's hand.

Ruth went over and peered at the skin. 'It looks like someone's carved something into the back of his hand.' The congealed blood made it difficult to see.

'Indeed,' Amis agreed. 'I had one of my technicians copy the exact line of the wound and they came up with this.' He clicked on his computer and an image appeared on the screen.

It looked like a word of some sort. There was a symbol that looked like a capital *P*. Then the lower case letters - *l*, *e* and a *u* that had a series of dots above. Finally, there was what looked like an exclamation mark with a squiggle at the bottom.

Ruth had no idea what they were looking at.

Taking his phone, Nick leaned over and took several photos of the symbols.

Ruth narrowed her eyes and looked at Amis. It was a bit spooky that the killer had taken the time to carve something on the back of Aaron's hand. 'Any idea what it means?'

'My first thought was that it was some sort of Gaelic or Celtic, but some of the lettering looks a little bit like the Greek alphabet too.'

Ruth shot a look over at Nick. The symbol had made her feel uneasy.

Chapter 16

French and Kennedy were driving out of Llancastell as they headed for the address they'd been given for PTC Security in Corwen. Since her arrival at Llancastell CID, French hadn't had much to do with Kennedy. Not for any other reason than he was usually partnered with DC Jim Garrow.

There was a slightly awkward silence in the car as they went around the roundabout that took them to the A5, the road that went west out through Llangollen to Corwen.

'How are you finding it?' French eventually asked. 'Being this side of the border, I mean.' He knew that they would be having one of those 'getting to know you' conversations which he always found unbearably awkward. He didn't do 'small talk' and avoided it as much as he could.

'Erm, it's mainly good. The big factor is having a decent SIO.'

SIO stood for Senior Investigating Officer, and in Ruth's case she was also head of CID.

French nodded in agreement. 'Yeah, the boss is spot

on. It wasn't that long ago that she got shot and we thought we were going to lose her.'

'I heard about that.'

'Lots of us thought she was going to retire after that, and then for selfish reasons you start thinking about who is going to replace her.'

'Nick? He seems to be her right-hand man here,' Kennedy said.

'Maybe. But he's not a DI,' French replied, 'and it would be very difficult to have a new DI landed on us from outside.'

'You get used to it,' Kennedy said unconvincingly.

French raised an eyebrow dubiously. 'Even DI Weaver?'

He was referring to the head of Chester CID with whom they'd worked recently over in Chester. Not only was it the general opinion that Weaver was a cock, he had hindered the murder investigation by pursuing his own agenda and ignoring vital evidence.

Kennedy gave a knowing laugh. 'Yeah, okay. DI Weaver is the exception. Chester Town Hall nick is the third CID I've worked at and Weaver was by far the worst DI.'

'Let's face it,' French said. 'He was a wanker.'

Kennedy cleared her throat. 'Erm, yes. I wouldn't have put it quite like that.'

French shrugged. 'You're in the North Wales Police now. You can say what you want about officers in Cheshire.'

Kennedy smiled at him. 'I suppose I can.'

'You sound like you've got a London accent,' he said as they sped along the road towards Llangollen.

'Streatham,' Kennedy said by way of an explanation.

French had a puzzled look on his face. He had no idea where that was.

'South London,' Kennedy explained.

'How did you end up in Chester?'

Kennedy gave him a bemused look.

'Sorry, I feel like I'm giving you the third degree,' he said apologetically.

'It's fine,' Kennedy reassured him. 'Where I grew up was very tough. Manor Park Estate. Lots of drugs, gangs and violence. Mum was on her own and I had three older brothers who got into a lot of trouble. Somehow I managed to get to Chester University to do a degree in criminology. And then I stayed.'

'Good for you,' French said, hoping he didn't sound patronising.

Within a few minutes they had slowed down and turned left over the bridge in central Llangollen. The pavements either side were heaving with tourists.

Kennedy opened the window and looked out. 'Lovely here, isn't it?'

'It is at this time of year,' French said as they crawled forward in the heavy traffic.

Kennedy looked over at him. She was now wearing some very cool looking sunglasses. 'I assume you're North Wales, born and bred?'

French laughed. 'That obvious is it?'

'Sorry, I didn't mean …'

'It's fine,' he reassured her. 'I'm proud of my roots.'

'Yeah, you should be. We all should be.'

French wasn't sure how to broach the next question. 'Do you mind if I ask you about your heritage, or is that crass?'

Kennedy smiled at him. 'No, that's fine. My great grandparents arrived on the SS Ormonde from Jamaica in 1947. In fact they arrived in Liverpool, but my great grandad didn't like it so they travelled down to South London.'

'Right,' French nodded, glad that he hadn't caused any offence. 'You ever been? To Jamaica?'

She shook her head. 'No. But I will do, one day. Maybe when I have kids.'

The traffic along the A5 had cleared, and the country-side over to the right was stunning in the summer sun.

'*Dod yn ol at fy nghoed*,' French said as he gestured over to the view.

Kennedy gave him a quizzical look.

'The actual translation is '… to return to my trees', but it means to find a sense of peace,' he explained. 'That's what I think when I look out and see that.'

'Very poetic.'

French shrugged with a grin. 'Hey, you're in Wales.'

Putting his foot down, they soon reached the bustling town of Corwen and came out the other side.

A sign on some metal fencing read – *PTC Security*.

Clicking the indicator, French turned left off the main road and along a dusty track that was full of bumps and potholes.

The track continued to wind and turn uphill for about half a mile before they came to some single-storey build-ings around a large concrete yard. It was surrounded by thick undergrowth and trees on all sides – Sitka spruce and Norwegian pines and larches.

There was a small car park to their right. A couple of pickup trucks and two old Land Rover Defender jeeps were parked there.

Getting out of the car, French felt the gentle breeze that swished through the nearby trees.

There was a long white Portakabin that had a small

wooden staircase leading up to a black door with *PTC Security – Enquiries* written on it.

'I guess we head over there,' Kennedy said as she slammed the passenger door shut and pointed at the door.

They walked across the yard, the dry stones and dirt crunching under their feet. It was so quiet, deserted and isolated that French thought it was a little unnerving.

He walked up the wooden stairs and gave the door an authoritative knock.

'Come in,' boomed a man's voice.

Opening the wooden door, French peered inside. There was an office with three desks. The walls were covered with military photos and adverts for PTC Security. They clearly offered their services all over the world.

'Hi there,' said a deep voice with a thick Welsh accent.

At a desk in the corner sat a thickset man with a shaved head and dark beard. As he stood up, French could see that he must have been around 6' 4". He was wearing a tight black PTC Security t-shirt, sand-coloured cargo trousers and Timberland boots.

French and Kennedy pulled out their warrant cards. 'Hi. Detective Sergeant French and Detective Constable Kennedy, Llancastell CID. I wonder if we could ask you a couple of questions?'

The man nodded with a friendly expression. 'Of course. Gary Williams,' he said, introducing himself and shaking their hands.

'We're making enquiries about a white BMW X5,' French said as he reached for his notebook. 'Registration STC 1000?'

'Yeah. It's one of our company cars,' he explained helpfully.

'Would you be able to tell us who was driving it on Monday?' Kennedy asked.

'Should do.' He beckoned them over to a desk, sat down and started to tap on the computer keyboard. Then he peered at the monitor. 'According to this, one of our directors, Ian Bellamy, was using it.' Then Gary gave them a quizzical look. 'Is everything all right?'

'Does the name Aaron Jenkins mean anything to you?' French asked.

Gary nodded immediately. 'Yes. I served in Afghanistan with Aaron in the Welsh Guards.'

'Have you seen him recently?' Kennedy enquired.

'Not for a couple of years. I know he lives locally but he keeps himself to himself these days to be honest. I think everything that happened over in Afghanistan really got to him.'

French gave an understanding nod. 'His brother Lee was killed over there, wasn't he?'

Gary nodded and gave them both a suspicious look. 'You've been doing your homework. What's all this about? Is Aaron all right?'

French took a moment and then said quietly, 'I'm afraid Aaron was murdered on Monday afternoon.'

Gary shook his head in disbelief. 'What? Murdered? I don't understand. What happened?'

Kennedy looked at him. 'I'm afraid we can't discuss the details of an ongoing investigation at this stage.'

'We believe that Ian Bellamy met with Aaron at The Red Lion pub on Monday lunchtime,' French explained. 'Do you know anything about that?'

Gary looked confused. 'Ian met up with Aaron?' he said in disbelief.

'You seem surprised?' Kennedy stated.

'I am. They fell out years ago. I didn't think they were even talking. The last time they were together was at Aaron's wedding and they ended up fighting.'

'We wondered if Ian might have been talking to Aaron about possible security work,' French said.

Gary didn't seem convinced. 'Maybe. But I'd be surprised … I'm sorry I can't be more helpful.'

'We're going to need some contact details for Ian Bellamy,' Kennedy said.

Gary pointed to his computer. 'No problem. I'll print them off for you now.'

Chapter 17

Ruth and Nick were making their way out of the car park of the hospital. Ruth was still mulling over the strange symbol they had seen carved into the back of Aaron Jenkins' hand. The last time she had seen anything like that was back in the spring of 2017. It had been when she'd first arrived at Llancastell CID and been launched straight into a murder case. A teacher had been strangled at a nearby school and then the headteacher had been murdered a few days later. Both of them had had ancient Celtic druid symbols of revenge carved into the back of their hands. Ruth had assumed that they were dealing with someone very disturbed – even a serial killer. However, the killer had turned out to be far closer to home. It was Nick's Uncle Mike, who blamed the teachers for his daughter's suicide. Mike admitted that he had carved the symbols on his victims' hands to throw the police off the scent.

'You thinking what I'm thinking?' Nick asked, breaking her train of thought.

'Which is what?'

'The last time we saw victims with something strange carved into their skin?'

'Yeah,' Ruth said quietly. 'I didn't want to bring it up.'

'It's fine,' Nick reassured her. 'Long time ago now. But it just reminded me that we shouldn't go too far down that rabbit hole.'

Ruth nodded in agreement. 'You mean it could be someone trying to throw us off the scent again?'

'Yeah.'

Her phone rang and she saw it was Llancastell CID.

'DI Hunter?' she said as she answered it.

'Boss,' said a voice. It was Georgie.

'What's going on?' Ruth asked her.

'I tracked down Natalie Jenkins' parents. They live in sheltered accommodation in Llandudno. I spoke to the warden there. Every visitor has to sign in and sign out. And guess what?'

'Go on,' Ruth said, but she had already guessed what Georgie was going to tell her.

'Natalie didn't visit her parents over the weekend. In fact she hasn't been up there in months.'

'Right,' Ruth said as she began to process what Georgie had told her. 'Good work, Georgie. See you later.'

Ruth ended the call and looked over at Nick.

'Everything all right?' he asked.

Ruth shook her head. 'No. Natalie Jenkins lied about her whereabouts yesterday. We need to go over to Manor Farm.'

Chapter 18

Garrow was sitting back in Court No 3. He could feel the anxiety in the pit of his stomach. The judge had spent the last hour talking to both the CPS and the defence team in his chambers. Garrow knew that it wasn't going to be good news.

'All rise,' said the court clerk.

Garrow stood as the judge came in through the wooden door to the side and made his way over to where he was sitting. The wall behind him was covered in dark grey slate with a huge Welsh coat of arms above that.

As the judge sat down, so did everyone else.

Garrow glanced around the courtroom. It wasn't as full as yesterday as it was just a preliminary hearing. There would be no jury until the case went to trial. And Garrow now feared that would never happen.

The judge looked down at some documents on the desk in front of him. He leaned over and spoke to one of the court clerks. Then he took off his glasses and cleaned them before looking out at the courtroom.

'After consultation with the CPS, and much deliberation,' he said, '… it is my opinion that there is no longer enough evidence for this case to proceed to a full trial. At this stage, it is my recommendation that the charges against Miss Lucy Morgan be dropped.'

Garrow's stomach lurched in dismay. He watched as Lucy grinned and then gave a little punch in the air.

The judge looked over at her. 'However, I must warn you Miss Morgan, that should more evidence against you materialise, the charges that the CPS brought against you can be reinstated and you will be rearrested. Do you understand that?'

Lucy nodded to confirm she understood.

'You are free to go,' the judge said.

Lucy turned and vigorously shook the hand of her defence counsel.

Garrow got up from where he was sitting quickly, making sure that he avoided any eye contact with either Lucy or Holloway.

Getting to the exit, he went out into the main corridor. He just wanted the ground to open up and swallow him.

He didn't think he'd ever felt this wretched in his life as he marched quickly towards the main entrance of the Mold Court building.

'DC Garrow?' called a voice.

It was Holloway who was marching down towards him.

Garrow gave him a quizzical look.

'I need a word with you in my office,' he said sternly.

Chapter 19

Ruth and Nick walked up to the front of the old stone farmhouse at Manor Farm and knocked on the black, thick oak door.

The young family liaison officer with the goatee beard answered.

'Just checking that Natalie is at home,' Ruth said to him.

'Yes, ma'am,' he replied. 'We got the okay from the SOCOs and forensics to come back here about two hours ago.'

'Is she on her own?' Nick asked.

The FLO nodded. 'She's in the kitchen, sarge.'

'Thank you, constable,' Ruth said as they headed down the hallway towards the kitchen.

The walls were painted white, with a few pictures and family photos hung in a line. There was a large photo of a man in military uniform. If Ruth was going to guess, it was taken in Afghanistan and the photo was of Aaron's brother, Lee.

The floors were made from dark stone, and the air

inside the farmhouse was bordering on chilly – which was refreshing after the heat outside.

Ruth spotted Natalie sitting at the long, oak kitchen table. There were pews either side. Over on the corner was a black AGA, and to the side of that a Welsh dresser. It was very similar to many of the farmhouse kitchens Ruth had visited since moving up to North Wales.

'Natalie?' Ruth said gently.

Natalie looked startled. 'Oh God, sorry. I was miles away.'

'I didn't mean to alarm you,' Ruth apologised as she and Nick came over to the table. 'There's a couple more things we need to go through with you.'

Natalie nodded. Her face was puffy from where she'd been crying. 'Yes, of course,' she whispered as she nursed a mug of tea. Her iPhone was on the table to one side.

'Okay if we sit down here?'

'Of course. Sorry. Yes. Do you want tea or coffee?' she asked them, although it sounded like a formality rather than a genuine offer.

Pulling out the pew so they could sit down, Nick shook his head. 'We're fine thanks,' he said politely.

Ruth sat forward on the pew and waited for a few seconds.

Natalie took a deep breath and looked at her. 'It just doesn't feel real.'

'No,' Ruth said empathetically. 'It's a very difficult time for you.'

'Do you have any idea when I'll get Aaron back?' Natalie asked. Then she shook her head. 'I can't believe that I'm even asking that question.'

'I'm afraid not. I know that there's been a preliminary post-mortem. And I can tell you that the cause of death is multiple gunshot wounds.'

Natalie nodded slowly. 'I've been going through it in my head. I just don't understand why anyone would shoot Aaron.'

Nick took out his notebook and turned a page. 'We just wanted to check something with you. You said that you'd spent the whole weekend over in Llandudno with your parents. Is that correct?'

'Yes,' she said, sounding a little defensive.

Ruth leaned forward and looked at her. *Why are you lying to us?*

'And you're sure about that?'

'Yes.' Natalie gave a nervous laugh and touched her face. 'Sorry, I don't understand.'

She's a terrible liar, Ruth thought.

Ruth waited for a few seconds for the tension to grow in the room. Natalie was lying to them about her whereabouts which was incredibly suspicious given that it coincided with her husband's murder.

Ruth made direct eye contact with her. 'We've spoken to the warden at Rose Meadow Court in Llandudno.'

Natalie tried not to react, but it was clear that this news had made her very uneasy.

'That is where your parents live isn't it?'

Natalie gave a virtually imperceptible nod as her eyes roamed anxiously around the room.

'Mr Casey, the warden at Rose Meadow Court, told us that every visitor has to sign in and out on every visit,' Ruth continued. 'The problem we have is that there is no record of you visiting your parents at the weekend.'

Natalie pulled a face as if this was absurd. 'What?'

'In fact, Mr Casey said you hadn't been to visit your parents for several months.'

'No,' Natalie shook her head but she looked rattled and frightened. 'He's made a mistake.'

Nick leaned forward. 'Why did you lie to us about where you were at the weekend, Natalie?'

'I didn't,' she protested, but her eyes filled with tears. 'I didn't.'

Ruth took a moment and pushed a stray strand of hair back over her ear. 'Whatever it is, Natalie, you can tell us,' she said in a comforting tone.

'We just need you to tell us the truth,' Nick reiterated.

Natalie put her hand to her face, shook her head and began to sob uncontrollably. Whatever it was, it was all too much for her.

Reaching into her pocket, Ruth took a tissue and handed it to her. 'Here you go,' she said quietly.

'Thank you,' Natalie whispered as she took the tissue and dabbed at her eyes.

They waited for a few more seconds for her to compose herself. She took a long, deep breath and then raised her head. Her eyes were watery and bloodshot.

'Could you tell us where you really were at the weekend, Natalie?' Nick asked gently.

If they were going to get her to tell them the truth, they needed what was referred to in the Met in the old days as '*the gentle touch*'.

She shook her head.

'You are going to have to tell us,' Ruth said calmly.

'I can't,' she cried anxiously. There were more tears in her eyes.

'Why not? Natalie, listen to me, you've lied about your whereabouts when Aaron was murdered. You do understand that it is very suspicious. So, we're going to need you to tell us what's going on or we're going to assume that you're involved.'

Natalie closed her eyes and took a long deep breath as if she was preparing herself to answer.

If Ruth had to guess, she presumed that Natalie had been with Charlie Jenkins. She had instinctively felt that there was something between them when they were interviewed.

Natalie looked away and bit her lip. 'I was at Charlie's house.'

'If you were at Charlie's house,' Ruth said in an innocent tone, '… why didn't you just tell us that?'

Ruth knew full well why she couldn't say anything. She had been sleeping with her brother-in-law at the time of her husband's murder. Natalie was racked by overwhelming guilt.

Natalie continued to look away and she shrugged. She looked completely lost.

'Is there something going on between you and Charlie, Natalie?' Ruth enquired in a low, quiet tone. She made sure that she avoided the word 'affair' at the moment. Ruth knew that the phrase '… something going on …' was far less disconcerting and it was easier to admit to.

Natalie closed her eyes again and nodded.

'And how long has it been going on?' Ruth asked in a tone that implied no judgement. She was there to find out the truth.

'A few months,' she whispered, and then the tears came again. Her body language and facial expression had changed, almost as if it had been a relief to finally admit to the affair.

'Did Aaron have any idea what was going on?' Nick asked.

'God no,' she replied. 'If he'd known, it would have …' Then she stopped herself finishing the sentence.

Ruth looked at her. 'Was it serious?'

Natalie spoke with no hesitation. 'Yes, I was going to

leave Aaron to be with Charlie. I couldn't take any more of Aaron's behaviour. It was all too much.'

'When you say 'Aaron's behaviour', what do you mean exactly?'

'He was so secretive, especially in the last year. I thought he was having an affair, but every time I confronted him about where he'd been or who he'd been talking to, he would explode in anger. He said that he was trying to save the farm and give us a better life.'

Nick frowned. 'What do you think he meant by that?'

'I've no idea. I assumed it was some kind of business deal but I don't know what.'

'Can you tell us where you were on Monday between 12pm and 4pm?' Ruth asked.

'I was at Charlie's house.'

'And Charlie was with you all day?' Nick asked to clarify.

'Yes, he went out to walk the dogs but that's all.'

'How long was he gone for?'

Natalie frowned suspiciously. 'About an hour. Maybe a bit longer.'

'And what time would that have been?'

'About half past one, I think.' It had clearly dawned on her that she had scuppered any chance of Charlie having an alibi.

'Thank you,' Ruth said in a compassionate tone.

Natalie looked at Ruth pleadingly. 'But Charlie didn't have anything to do with what happened to Aaron. I know he didn't.'

Ruth exchanged a look with Nick. If Aaron was murdered at 2pm, then Charlie was out and had no alibi for the time of his brother's death. And he was having an affair with his wife.

Chapter 20

Kennedy was now driving as they entered Llangollen on their way east from Corwen along the A5. After a few minutes, she pulled into a road on the north side of Llangollen. It was the address that Gary Williams had given them for Ian Bellamy. They wanted to find out why he had met with Aaron Jenkins at The Red Lion pub on Monday and what they had talked about. It certainly seemed suspicious given what Gary Williams had told them about Bellamy and Aaron's relationship. Plus, Bellamy might well have been the last person to see Aaron alive – except for the killer.

French looked at the address on the printout that Gary Williams had given him and then saw No 6 to their left.

'This is it,' he said as he unclipped his seat belt.

'Hold on a second,' Kennedy said very quietly as she looked in the rear-view mirror. 'Don't look round, but I think that Ian Bellamy is behind us.'

'Okay.' French manoeuvred himself so that he could look into the wing mirror.

A white BMW X5 had pulled over to the pavement about thirty yards behind them and parked.

French frowned. 'I wonder why he's not parking on his drive?'

A figure got out.

It was a man in his 40s – sunglasses, black baseball cap.

It was the man from the CCTV that Ruth and Nick had found at The Red Lion pub.

'Stroke of luck,' Kennedy muttered under her breath as she opened the driver's door and got out.

French got out, turned, and pulled out his warrant card. 'Ian Bellamy?'

Looking instantly startled, Bellamy turned sharply and sprinted back to his car.

Are you joking?

'Bollocks,' French growled, 'he's doing a bloody runner.'

Kennedy and French immediately jumped back in their car.

French heard the sound of a car engine revving. He glanced in the wing mirror and saw the BMW begin to pull away from the pavement at high speed.

Turning on the ignition, Kennedy gunned the 2-litre fuel injection engine.

'No chance, sunshine!' she snarled as she suddenly pulled their black Astra across the road to block Bellamy's escape path.

Turning around, French saw the BMW lurch to a sudden halt.

The road was far too narrow to do a nifty U-turn or even a three-point turn. And that meant Bellamy was stuck.

'Nice one,' French said, impressed by Kennedy's quick thinking.

With a roar, the BMW reversed backwards at high speed and then came to another sudden halt.

And then French had a sinking feeling that Bellamy wasn't about to get out of his car and talk to them quietly.

'Shit!' he muttered under his breath.

Kennedy frowned. 'You don't think he's going to …?'

'Yeah, I think that's exactly what he's going to do.'

Before they could react, the BMW sped at them and smashed into the left-hand wing of the car, knocking them back towards the pavement and out of the way.

There was a huge bang inside the car and the sound of metal crunching and glass smashing.

French felt himself jolt suddenly to his right and then as he came back the other way, his head hit the door frame.

He saw stars, and a searing pain shot through his head. 'Shit!' he gasped.

'For fuck's sake!' Kennedy yelled in anger. 'Are you okay?'

'I think so,' he said, but his head was still ringing.

He took a moment to compose himself.

'Right, we're having that bastard!' Kennedy snapped as she stamped down on the accelerator with such force that the car jolted forward. The tyres squealed under them with the sudden burst of speed.

French was thrown back in his seat by the force of the acceleration.

'Okay,' he said in a cautionary tone. His head was still fuzzy. 'Let's just take it nice and easy, eh?'

He could see how angry and indignant Kennedy was as she gripped the steering wheel.

Grabbing the car's Tetra radio, French clicked the grey *Talk* button. 'Control from eight zero, are you receiving, over?'

After a few seconds there was a crackle and a male voice. 'Eight zero, this is Control, we are receiving, go ahead.'

Kennedy accelerated up to 50mph as they sped up the road and spotted the BMW turning left and then disappearing.

'We're in pursuit of a white BMW X5, registered to PTC Security, based in Corwen,' French explained as they screamed towards the junction with the main road and then came to a shuddering halt. 'Registration Papa, Tango, Charlie, one, zero, zero, zero. Repeat, registration Papa, Tango, Charlie, one, zero, zero, zero.'

French glanced at the built-in satnav map. 'We're heading north on the A542, coming out of Llangollen. Request back up, over.'

'Eight zero, received, stand by,' the computer aided dispatch controller said.

Darting out onto the other side of the road, Kennedy reached over and switched on the siren and the blue lights – known as *the blues and twos* - that were located in the radiator grill.

'Right, everyone get out of my bloody way,' she said with grim determination.

A bus tried to pull out from a bus stop to their left.

'You can stay there,' she snapped as she stamped on the brake and swerved left to avoid it.

French was thrown hard against his seat belt and then back by the force of Kennedy's braking.

'Where the hell did you learn to drive?' he asked, his eyes widening. 'On a PlayStation?'

Kennedy shrugged. 'South London. Sorry, but I'm not letting him get away. He bloody rammed us.'

The BMW was up ahead and weaving in and out of the traffic at speed.

As French looked out, he saw the BMW pull out to overtake a caravan.

A lorry was coming the other way.

Jesus, he's not going to make that, he thought to himself.

They both watched in horror as the BMW tried to swerve back over but instead clipped the lorry.

'Shit!' Kennedy gasped as they slowed down.

The BMW flipped over. And then over again, before skidding along the road on its roof. Sparks flew up from where the metal roof grated along the tarmac surface.

Kennedy brought the car to a sudden stop. She and French flung open the doors. Several other cars had swerved to avoid the BMW and were now stopped on the road.

Breaking into a sprint, they ran to the car. The wheels were still spinning and there was smoke coming from the engine.

Bellamy was upside down and clearly unconscious. He had a bloody gash across his temple.

French crouched down and pulled the handle on the driver's door. It was either locked or jammed.

'Control, this is eight zero, are you receiving, over? Kennedy said with urgency into her radio.

'Eight zero, this is Control, receiving, go ahead.'

French went around to the passenger door, crouched down and pulled on the handle.

The door opened.

He was instantly hit by the strong smell of petrol.

Shit, this is not good.

'We have a serious RTA and need paramedics urgently,' Kennedy explained. 'We also need a fire engine with cutting equipment. Our current location is the A542, around six miles north of Llangollen, over.'

'Received, eight zero, stand by.'

French crawled into the upside-down BMW and got over to the driver's side.

Kennedy looked in at him with concern. 'I can smell petrol.'

French nodded. 'We're going to need to get him out quickly.'

He then reached for the seat belt's red release button. However, he knew that once he pressed it, Bellamy would fall out of the driver's seat and down against the windscreen and dashboard. If he had any neck or spinal injury, it could make it a hundred times worse. But there wasn't time to wait for the cutting equipment as it smelled as if the petrol tank had been fractured, and one spark from the engine or a wire would see the car go up in a ball of flames.

Here goes, French thought as he released the button.

Bellamy's unconscious body fell from the seat and crashed against the shattered windscreen and upturned roof.

Reaching across, French grabbed his jacket with both hands and pulled as hard as he could.

Bellamy groaned as French pulled him towards the passenger door.

'Here,' Kennedy said, reaching in and helping to pull.

After a few seconds, they managed to drag Bellamy out of the car and onto the road.

The smell of petrol was getting stronger.

French looked at Kennedy. 'We need to get him away from this car right now,' he said urgently.

They pulled him across the road and onto a grassy verge.

BANG!

Suddenly, the BMW exploded in a huge ball of orange flames.

French and Kennedy looked at each other – *Jesus that was close!*

Putting his fingers to Bellamy's neck, French could feel a faint pulse. 'Yeah, he's still alive.'

Chapter 21

Having had a dressing down yet again from Holloway, Garrow now made his way slowly out of the Mold Court building. He walked down the stone steps and headed left towards the rear car park.

Taking out his sunglasses, he put them on as he took his car keys from his trouser pocket. As he got to the driver's door, he saw in the reflection of the glass that someone was walking up behind him.

'Thank you,' said a cheery voice that he recognised.

His stomach muscles clenched with anxiety.

Garrow turned to see that it was Lucy Morgan.

Jesus.

She was wearing 70s Boho sunglasses, which she took off and then peered at him with a bemused smile.

'You don't seem pleased to see me,' she laughed.

Garrow frowned and mumbled, 'I need to go.'

Feeling very uneasy, he opened the driver's door.

'Oh dear. Running away like a little boy,' she taunted him with a disappointed face. 'Well off you go then, Jim.'

He stopped for a moment and tried to compose himself, then turned back to look at her.

'What do you want?' he asked quietly. He glanced around the car park, but it seemed to be deserted. He certainly didn't want anyone to spot him talking to Lucy after what had just happened.

'What do I want?' she snorted as she pushed the sunglasses into her hair on top of her head. 'I just told you. I wanted to thank you. If you hadn't decided to come in that day and have a glass of wine, I'd be going to prison for twenty years now.'

'So, you've come to gloat?' he asked in a withering tone. There was a voice in his head that was warning him not to get into a conversation and to get in the car and drive away. But the other voice wanted to find out what she was thinking, and why she had come to speak to him.

'Gloat? I don't do gloating, Jim,' she said, shaking her head, 'but you know that.' Her tone was so incredibly over-familiar that it was creepy.

'But I don't know do I?' he said with a deliberately cautious voice. 'Because I don't know you, do I?'

'Don't be ridiculous,' she scoffed. 'You do know me. You know what we had was special. You can't fake that kind of thing, can you?'

Oh God, she is seriously delusional, he thought to himself.

'I'm pretty sure that it was you who was faking, Lucy,' he said calmly. 'When I got to know you, you had conveniently forgotten to tell me the bit about you brutally murdering your mother and then faking amnesia. Or have you forgotten?'

'You knew what I'd done all along,' she protested. 'Don't pretend you hadn't worked all that out, silly. You're an incredible detective.'

'Right,' Garrow said decisively. He had no interest in

listening to the thoughts of a mad woman whose lies had probably cost him his job.

'Jim?'

'Yes?' he replied frustratedly.

'I will find a way of thanking you properly. Very soon. After all, I know where you live.'

Garrow could feel his pulse quicken. *Does she really know where I live?* he wondered anxiously.

Getting into his car, he slammed the door angrily. He was furious at Lucy for what she'd done. And he was furious that he'd allowed himself to be drawn into a conversation with her.

Starting the ignition, he reversed the car out of the parking space. Then put the car into first gear.

As he drove slowly towards the exit, Lucy put her sunglasses back on and gave him a friendly wave.

For a fleeting second, Garrow imagined driving the car into Lucy so that she would be out of his life forever.

Then he put that thought out of his head as he pulled out of the car park and sped away.

Chapter 22

Ruth and Nick had tracked Charlie Jenkins down to an industrial estate between Llangollen and Wrexham, where he owned a company called *Jenkins Fences and Sheds Ltd*.

Pulling into the large car park, Ruth squinted as the late afternoon sun dazzled her through the windscreen. The car radio was on very low, but she caught the opening bars to *Roy Ayers'* summer classic *Everybody Loves the Sunshine*.

Reaching over, she turned up the volume.

'Now this is a tune,' she said with a smile.

'Roy Ayers, isn't it?'

'Yeah, all right clever clogs,' she moaned. 'Sarah and I saw him at Glastonbury in the early noughties. We'd had some hash cake. The sun was setting behind the Jazz Stage. It was just perfect.'

Nick laughed. 'Just when I think there's no hope for you, you tell me a story like that which revives my hope that you're not a lost cause.'

'Oh, piss off, you patronising nob,' she said with a grin. She was used to Nick's snobbery when it came to music. And his arrogance.

She sang along for a few bars. '*My life, my life, my life, in the sunshine …*'

Nick rolled his eyes as he opened the driver's door. 'Come on, you old hippy. We are actually working.'

'Oi, less of the old,' Ruth replied as she got out.

Over to their right was a large wooden shed that had been converted into a showroom and offices. A large sign read *Customers' Entrance*.

As soon as they walked in, Ruth spotted Charlie Jenkins sitting in the small glass-walled office. He looked lost in thought. She was surprised that he had come to work given what had happened to his brother two days ago.

He clearly spotted their arrival as he looked up. His face fell.

Ruth went to the half-open door and looked in. 'Okay if we come in? We just need to go through a few things.'

Charlie held up his hands in an appeasing gesture. 'It's okay. Natalie phoned me to tell me about what she'd told you earlier.'

Ruth and Nick entered the office, went over to two chairs, and sat down.

'I'm not proud of what we've done,' Charlie babbled nervously, '… but you need to know that I'd never do anything to harm my brother.'

Ruth looked over at him. 'You and Natalie both lied about her whereabouts on Monday. And that makes us suspicious.'

'I understand that.' Charlie shook his head. 'We just didn't want to admit that we were having an affair behind Aaron's back,' he sighed.

Nick, who had taken out his notebook and pen, said, 'We're going to need you to tell us where you were between 12pm and 4pm on Monday afternoon.'

Charlie gave an innocent shrug. 'I was at home with Natalie.'

Well, that's a lie for starters.

Ruth gave him a quizzical look. 'All afternoon?' she asked in a dubious tone.

'Yes,' Charlie replied immediately. Then something occurred to him. 'Oh, actually no. I went out to walk the dogs at one point.'

'On your own?' Nick asked.

Charlie nodded and frowned. 'Yes.'

Ruth narrowed her eyes. 'Natalie didn't want to come with you?'

'She was having a nap,' he explained casually.

'Did you see anyone or talk to anyone while you were out walking the dogs?' Nick enquired.

'No,' Charlie replied, but he seemed to be getting increasingly nervous. 'But I didn't go anywhere. Just around the block. And I didn't have anything to do with what happened to Aaron. He was my brother.'

Ruth waited for a few seconds. Her instinct was that Charlie was telling them the truth.

'Look, there is something,' Charlie said. 'You asked Natalie about Aaron's gun cabinet this morning.'

Ruth nodded. 'Yes.'

'A few months ago, Aaron and I got drunk up at the farmhouse. He went to the gun cabinet and pulled out a Skorpion submachine gun.'

Ruth and Nick exchanged a look.

'I think he was showing off,' Charlie said.

'Did you ask him about it?' Nick asked.

'Yeah. He said he was looking after it for some 'very dangerous' people.'

'Did he say anything else?'

'No. He put it back, and when I asked him who they were he just told me that it was better that I didn't know.'

Ruth raised an eyebrow. 'Why didn't you mention this earlier?'

'I don't know. I suppose I didn't want it to come out that Aaron was mixed up in anything illegal.'

'Right,' Ruth said. Although holding on to a machine gun for some very dangerous people was incredibly vague, it did give them a clue as to what Aaron had been doing in recent months – and what type of company he'd been keeping. And it also might provide a clue as to why his life might have been in danger.

As Ruth got up to go, she thought of something else. 'There is just one more thing. Do you think Aaron had any idea that you and Natalie were having an affair?'

Charlie shook his head. 'I know that he didn't actually.'

'How can you be so sure of that?'

'The same night that Aaron showed me the Skorpion, he also told me he was having an affair. He made me promise not to tell anyone.'

Nick stopped writing and looked over at him with a curious expression. 'Did he tell you who he was having an affair with?'

Charlie nodded but didn't say anything.

Ruth looked directly at him. 'You have to tell us, Charlie.'

'Aaron was sleeping with Bethan who works in The Red Lion,' he said reluctantly.

Chapter 23

It was dark outside as Garrow went out of the living room and made his way down the hallway to his kitchen. The anxiety of the day was still lying deep in his gut. It felt like there was a tight knot in his stomach that wouldn't go away.

He went to the cupboard and took out a bottle of Jameson whiskey. It was nearly full. Garrow wasn't much of a drinker. He didn't like the feeling of being out of control. If he drank anything, then it would be a few pints of bitter or real ale.

Opening the freezer door, he reached in and took out an ice tray. He grabbed a heavy glass tumbler. Twisting the tray, he took out a handful of ice cubes which he dropped into the glass with a satisfying clunk. Then he twisted open the top of the whiskey and poured in a decent measure. If he was to guess, it was at least a treble. He didn't care. He just wanted the anxiety to go. Self-medicating with whiskey wasn't the best idea, but he felt desperate.

He swilled the whiskey and ice for a few seconds and then took a mouthful. It instantly burned the back of his throat, and he could smell the powerful fumes going up his nostrils. It was so strong that his eyes watered and he made a guttural sound.

Jesus, that is deeply unpleasant.

Garrow wondered how so many characters he watched on television – especially in old British films or American cop shows – just seemed to drink whiskey all day as if it was just a harmless cup of tea. The stuff tasted like diesel to him and was disgusting.

Fuck it, he thought as he held his breath and threw back the rest of the glass. He wasn't drinking the stuff for the taste. He wanted the effect.

He poured himself another measure and ambled back out of the kitchen, down the hallway and into the living room. There was a political programme on the television with politicians arguing. Politics wasn't his thing, so he turned it off. He found mainstream politics and politicians deeply depressing. He was a socialist at heart but he knew that the country would never elect a truly socialist prime minister or government. Therefore there was little point in taking much interest.

He went over to his turntable and began to thumb through his records. His taste in music was eclectic to say the least. Everything from *The Beatles* to *Bach*. He spotted a *John Coltrane* album – *Blue Train: The Complete Masters*.

That was perfect. A bit of melancholy jazz that would complement his feelings of self-pity and worry. The photo of John Coltrane looked like he felt. His favourite track on the album was *I'm Old Fashioned* which he thought was incredibly apt. He'd always felt like a fogey. One of his friends said he'd been born a fogey. While most students at university were out taking drugs and dancing, Garrow had spent his evenings drinking ale in a local pub, playing chess, or talking about everything from literature to science.

There was a sudden knock at the door which made him jump.

Even though the whiskey had given him a warm glow that seemed to emanate from his stomach, he was still feeling twitchy.

Glancing at his watch, he saw that it was 10.30pm. He wasn't expecting anyone.

He put down his glass of whiskey and padded down the hallway to the front door.

For a second, he thought of Lucy Morgan and her parting words that she knew where he lived.

It seemed sensible not to open the door.

'Hello?' he called.

Silence.

He wished he had a spy hole on his front door.

Crouching down, he hooked his finger as quietly as he could around the metallic letter box and pulled it gently back.

For a split second, he saw that someone was there but opening the letter box had clearly alerted them. Before he could see anything more than a figure, they'd gone.

This is not good, he thought to himself.

'Hello?' he asked again.

His heart was now thumping against his chest.

Taking a breath to compose himself, he stood up and then turned the key in the lock of the door and removed the key.

With his mind racing, he walked slowly down the hallway and back into the living room. What was going on? It was too late for kids to be pranking by knocking on the door and running away. He wasn't expecting any deliveries.

The only explanation he could think of was that Lucy had knocked on his door. What did she want? Did she want to scare him, or worse?

He swigged back the rest of his whiskey.

Out of the corner of his eye, he saw something moving in his garden through the patio doors that led outside.

What the hell was that?

His anxiety was now through the roof.

Or was it just his imagination? Was he being completely paranoid?

He went to the wall, turned off the main lights and then moved cautiously to the patio doors.

Taking another breath, he moved close to the glass to look outside.

His small, neat garden was shadowy. A streetlight over the back cast a vanilla hue.

His eyes scanned left and right.

Nothing.

The garden was empty.

Maybe it really was my imagination. Phew.

He sighed and turned back.

It was time to head upstairs and go to bed.

BANG!

There was a sudden THUD against the glass.

Garrow spun around.

Lucy Morgan's face was pressed against the glass with a terrifying grin.

Jesus Christ!

He jumped out of his skin.

Lucy gave a laugh as she made eye contact with him.

Then she turned and disappeared into the darkness of the garden.

Chapter 24

It was early morning and Ruth had put her feet up on her desk as she pushed back in her office chair. She pulled her toes back on her right foot to stretch out her right calf which felt a little tight. She had already received a text from Garrow to explain that the charges against Lucy Morgan had been dropped by the CPS on the recommendation of the judge. He also explained that he was feeling very under the weather and would be unable to come to work today. Ruth was concerned, as she had never known Garrow to ever have time off work due to illness. And the fact that it was the day after the events at Mold Court was a worry. She made a mental note to call him later and check that he was okay.

Her eye was drawn over to the framed photo of Daniel which she had on her desk. His cheeky smile which beamed from under his baseball cap melted her heart. She had no idea what she'd do if they didn't get to adopt him. There was no way that social services would allow her and Sarah to keep Daniel at their home indefinitely on a temporary fostering licence. What if someone more suitable than her and Sarah came on the scene and wanted to adopt Daniel instead? The thought made her feel sick. She told herself that she was catastrophising and to put it out of her mind. But catastrophising is what she did.

Last week she'd found a mole under her armpit and was convinced that it had grown. Within minutes she was certain that it was skin cancer and was planning her funeral. She'd reiterated to Sarah that she wanted *Wham!'s* '*Edge of Heaven*' played at the end of the service. But then Sarah assured her that she'd seen that very mole before, and it looked exactly the same as it did years ago.

As Ruth's eyes moved across her desk, they rested on the photo of her daughter Ella. Now in her mid-20s, she and Ella were close, although she'd seen slightly less of her in the past year. Work and a new boyfriend kept Ella busy, but Ruth didn't mind as long as she was happy.

Taking her legs down from the desk, she realised that she had pins and needles in her left foot, and it was now numb. She tried to wiggle her toes and stamp her foot until the feeling returned.

She checked her watch. 8am. She'd been in her office for nearly two hours already. She could see that the CID team was assembling for the morning briefing. *Here we go again,* she thought to herself as she grabbed her coffee and the case folders and headed out of her office.

'Morning everyone,' she said loudly as she headed for the scene board that had been set up on the far side of the office. There was a central photograph of Aaron Jenkins that had been lifted from his social media. The date, location and cause of death was scribbled in black marker pen underneath. There were various other photos dotted around along with a map of the area. The location of the murder was signified by a red pin. 'Right let's get going please.' Ruth pointed to a photograph. 'This is our victim,

Aaron Jenkins. Shot and killed on Monday afternoon at close range with a submachine gun in a field on Manor Farm. An eyewitness describes seeing a figure in a black baseball cap carrying out the shooting. Nick?'

Nick got up from where he was sitting and went over to the scene board. 'We know that Aaron Jenkins had recently filed for bankruptcy. Manor Farm was losing money and there were outstanding bills and tax.' He pointed to a photo. 'His wife, Natalie, works as a local primary school teacher. She claims to have had no knowledge of the state of the farm's finances. Natalie claimed that she was with her parents over in Llandudno all weekend. However, we have discovered that she is having an affair with Charlie Jenkins, Aaron's younger brother, who lives a few miles away in Llangollen.'

Georgie frowned. 'Do they have alibis?'

Nick shook his head. 'No. Natalie claims that she was at Charlie's house at the time of Aaron's murder. Charlie admits that he was walking his dogs at this time, but he has no one to corroborate his story.'

Ruth pointed to another photograph. 'And this is made more complicated as Aaron told Charlie that he was having an affair with Bethan Jones who works at The Red Lion pub.'

French leaned back in his chair, his hands behind his head. 'That is a tangled web.'

'As we know, Aaron met this man,' Nick said, gesturing to the first of two images, 'Ian Bellamy. Aaron and Bellamy both served together in the Welsh Guards and did two tours of Afghanistan in 2007 and 2009. Bellamy works for PTC Security, which is owned by this man, Gary Williams, who also served with Bellamy and Aaron.'

'What do PTC Security do?' Georgie asked.

'They employ ex-military for security jobs all over the world.'

French narrowed his eyes. 'Mercenaries?'

'We're not sure. My suspicion is that Aaron had fallen on hard times and so he contacted Bellamy at PTC to see if there was any work going. That's why they met at The Red Lion on Monday lunchtime. However, we are also aware that Aaron and Bellamy did not get on and hadn't spoken for a long time.'

Ruth got up from where she was perched on the edge of a table. 'We have an empty gun cabinet in Aaron's farmhouse along with a box of 9mm ammunition. Plus, Charlie told us that Aaron had shown him a Czech-made Skorpion machine gun that he told his brother he was keeping for some 'very dangerous' people.'

Kennedy sat forward in her seat. 'Do we know what ammunition the Skorpion uses?'

'9mm, and the bullets that were retrieved from Aaron's body have also been confirmed by forensics as 9mm too.'

'So, he might have been killed by the gun that he was 'keeping' for someone else?' Georgie suggested.

'It's definitely possible.' Ruth then pointed to the photos of the back of Aaron's hand. 'The one thing that confuses me a little is this carving. Bottle of champagne to anyone who can work out what that symbol or lettering means. Dan?'

French shifted forward in his seat. 'Jade and I went to question Bellamy about his meeting with Aaron in The Red Lion pub. He got spooked and did a runner. It ended with him being involved in an RTA. He's now in Llancastell University Hospital in a coma. We're not sure how serious his injuries are but he is stable. Overnight we secured a search warrant for his home, so we hope that might give us a clue as to why he was so alarmed by us showing up yesterday.'

Ruth nodded as she took all this in. 'That's great work guys. Can we do some background checks on Bethan Jones and Haji Rafiq please.' She took a breath. 'Right, let's get to work.'

Chapter 25

An hour later, Ruth and Nick were making their way from Llancastell towards Llangollen and then on to The Red Lion pub. If Bethan Jones had been having an affair with Aaron, they needed to speak to her. Even though Ruth was now convinced that Aaron's murder was somehow connected to the Skorpion gun he was 'keeping safe' for someone, an affair needed the investigation to run on a TIE basis. It was a police acronym for *Trace*, *Interview* and then *Eliminate*. That meant talking to everyone in Aaron's life to see if they could be ruled out of being involved in his death.

Buzzing down the window, Ruth moved to her left and let the warm summer air rush against her face and stream through her hair. She took a deep breath and let out a sigh.

'You can't do this on the South Circular,' she said.

Nick frowned. 'I assume that the South Circular is a very busy road in London?'

'Yes, it's bloody horrible. And on a day like this we'd be stuck in traffic with fumes everywhere. The heat traps the pollution. It's hideous.'

Nick gave her a quizzical look. 'It's funny. You used to talk about London when you first came up here. Obviously. But now you hardly mention it.'

Ruth shrugged. 'This is home,' she explained casually.

'You really think that now?' Nick asked with genuine curiousity.

'I do.'

'You'd never go back then?'

Ruth shook her head. 'God, no.' She pointed out at the stunning landscape of North Wales to their right. 'Look at this. I'd be mad to ever leave.'

Nick gave a bemused smile.

'What?'

'Nothing.'

'Go on,' she prompted him.

'I suppose as a Welshman, I take some pride that you've come here and you love it so much that it's now your adopted home.'

Ruth took a cigarette from the packet that she'd taken from the glove compartment. 'I'm getting old,' she said. 'I like a quieter pace of life.'

She lit her cigarette and then blew the smoke out of the window.

'Yeah, although you're kind of ruining the whole fresh country air vibe by smoking that,' Nick quipped sardonically.

Ruth laughed. 'Bugger off.'

Nick started to indicate left and they pulled into the car park of The Red Lion which was virtually empty.

Getting out of the car, Ruth took a drag of her cigarette. 'I didn't time that very well, did I?' she said, holding the virtually intact cigarette up before stubbing it out.

'No comment,' Nick said as he closed the driver's door.

They made their way across the car park and into the pub which had just opened.

It was empty.

Spotting Haji behind the bar, Ruth and Nick approached.

He was clearly bottling up and distracted. He was wearing a red retro Moroccan football shirt with the name *Naybet* printed on the back.

'Hi, Haji,' Ruth said as they got to the bar.

It seemed to make him jump.

'Oh God, sorry,' he said apologetically. 'I didn't even hear you come in.'

'Is Bethan around?' Nick asked.

Haji shook his head. 'She doesn't start until lunchtime.'

'We're going to need an address for her.'

'Erm, okay. Of course,' he said helpfully. 'It should be on the computer in the office.'

'Actually,' Ruth said, 'while we're here, Aaron Jenkins was a regular at this pub, wasn't he?'

'Yes, he was in here most days.'

'How did he seem in recent weeks when he came in?'

Haji took a moment to think and then said, 'A bit quiet actually. You know, distracted.'

'Did he ever say anything that might give us a clue as to why he was feeling like that?'

Haji shrugged and then shook his head. 'Not really. He kept himself to himself, except when he was drinking and playing darts. Then he could get a bit rowdy.'

Ruth narrowed her eyes. 'Did you ever seen him in here with anyone you didn't recognise or who seemed out of place?'

For a second Haji didn't reply but then he thought of something. 'Actually, yes. About four or five weeks ago he was in here with some blokes. I'd never seen them before, and they looked …' Haji searched for the right word, '… a bit scary.'

'Scary? How do you mean?'

'Big blokes, shaved heads, tracksuits.'

'Anything else?' Nick asked.

'They were from Liverpool. I heard their accents.'

Ruth looked at Nick. They knew that Aaron had been holding a submachine gun for people who he had described to his brother Charlie as 'dangerous'. Maybe these were the people he was talking about.

'Would you happen to have the CCTV for that day?' Ruth asked hopefully.

Haji furrowed his brow. 'Actually I think I might be able to narrow it down. Liverpool were playing a pre-season friendly, and Aaron asked if I could put it up on the TV.'

'Can you remember the game?'

Grabbing hold of his phone, Haji started to look. Then he pointed at the screen. 'This is it. Liverpool v Bayern Munich in Singapore. August 2nd.'

'Does that mean you've got the CCTV from that day?'

'Yes. We only dump the CCTV stuff on the first of the month.'

Nick gestured over to the door. 'Okay if we have a look?'

'Of course. I can show you.'

As they had done before, Ruth and Nick went behind the bar and followed Haji into the small office where he sat down behind the computer. He switched it on, waited for it to load, and started to click on CCTV files.

'I like your shirt,' Nick said.

'Oh right, yeah,' Haji said with a self-conscious laugh.

'Naybet. He played for Tottenham, didn't he?'

Haji widened his eyes. 'That's right,' he said with a

surprised smile. 'I liked him when he was at Deportivo.' He clicked a file marked *2.8.21*. 'Here we go.'

CCTV from that day came onto the screen and Haji played it forward at high speed until the timecode reached *7.00pm*. Then he slowed it down until he saw a car driving into the car park.

'I think this is them,' he said, pointing to a black Range Rover Sport with tinted windows.

Ruth watched as the Range Rover parked and two men got out.

As Haji had described, they were in their 30s, thickset, shaved heads and were wearing designer sportswear and sunglasses.

They couldn't look more like members of an OCG if they tried, Ruth thought to herself dryly. *And a black Range Rover Sport to top it all.*

'Jesus,' Nick said under his breath, 'they look friendly.'

Ruth pointed to the screen. 'Can you freeze it for a second, please?'

Nick took out his notepad and pen and scribbled down the registration. 'Let's see what the DVLA comes up with.'

Ruth looked at Haji. 'Did you ever see them in here again?'

'No. I don't know if it's important but I think they came from Birkenhead.'

'Why do you say that?'

'When they were at the bar they were talking, and one of them said, *Birkenhead to here in 50 minutes. Better than last time when you drove.* And the other one said, *Yeah, that's because you drive like a dickhead.*'

Chapter 26

French and Kennedy were standing outside a detached white house in Dinbren Road in Llangollen. It was the address they had parked outside the previous day until Bellamy had rammed them and driven off. Kennedy had just called the University Hospital in Llancastell and Bellamy was still in a critical condition in the intensive care unit.

There were only houses on one side of Dinbren Road. On the other side there was a large park with a playing field and goals, and beyond that the land rose up to a hill blanketed by trees.

French signalled to two uniformed officers to join them at the front door. They had arranged a Section 18 Search Warrant, so the plan was that if there was no reply they would use a battering ram – known by the police as 'the big red key' – to make a forced entry.

French stepped forward and gave an authoritative knock on the door. Then he took the warrant from his pocket.

There were a few seconds of silence. All they could hear was the sound of children playing over in the park.

French looked at Kennedy and shrugged.

She gestured to a ground floor window. 'I'll go and have a look.'

Crouching down, French pushed the letterbox open and peered inside. There were no signs of movement.

He then glanced over at Kennedy who had cupped her hands to look through the ground floor window. She looked back over at him and shook her head.

'No, sarge. Nothing.'

French gave the signal to the uniformed officers. 'Right guys, let's get this door open please.'

He took two steps back.

The officers swung the heavy steel battering ram against the door.

CRACK!

The front door flew open with a bang.

'Police!' the first uniformed officer shouted as they went inside.

'Police! Show yourself please!' the other officer shouted.

French and Kennedy followed them inside.

The house was basic but nicely furnished. It smelled of air freshener or furniture polish.

'You guys check upstairs,' French said to the uniformed officers who then thundered up the staircase noisily.

French marched down the hallway, checking rooms as he went.

'Clear,' he shouted as he looked in the living room.

'Sarge,' Kennedy called from the large kitchen at the rear of the property.

'What is it?' he asked as he entered.

The kitchen was new and high spec. It was white with

a large table, rolled marble tops, a Rangemaster cooker and a kitchen island surrounded by chrome stools.

Whatever Bellamy is into, he's making a decent living doing it, French thought to himself.

Kennedy gestured to a steel gun cabinet on the side wall. 'I'm guessing we should check this,' she suggested.

French went over and twisted the handle but it was locked.

'All clear upstairs, sarge,' one uniformed officer said as they came into the kitchen.

'Good.' French pointed to the gun cabinet. 'We're going to need to get that open, guys.'

'Right you are.' The officer reached to the tool belt he was wearing and pulled up a small iron crowbar. He then stepped forward, put the crowbar into the door and yanked it hard.

Nothing.

He tried it again and the gun cabinet door flew open.

Inside were half a dozen semi-automatic weapons.

'Jesus Christ,' French said under his breath. It was like a military armoury.

Chapter 27

Ruth knocked on the front door of a small house which was the address they'd been given for Bethan Jones in Llangollen. It was a little ramshackle with flaky paint, and the path to the front door was strewn with weeds.

The door opened and Bethan looked out. The blood visibly drained from her face.

'Hi Bethan,' Ruth said in a friendly tone. 'Do you mind if we come in for a moment. There's a few things we'd just like to go through with you. It won't take more than a few minutes.'

Bethan nodded but she looked incredibly nervous as she reluctantly opened the front door fully to allow Ruth and Nick to come inside.

'Do you want to come through to the kitchen?' she asked quietly.

'Yes. Sounds good.'

Ruth could smell stale tobacco, and the air smelled damp despite the hot weather outside. She assumed that Bethan shared the house with a male friend or even a boyfriend judging by the coats and shoes that were lined up along the hallway.

As they went into the small dark kitchen, Bethan looked at them anxiously. 'Erm, do you want a drink?'

Ruth gave her a friendly smile. 'We're fine thanks.'

They pulled out chairs that were around a scruffy circular table and sat down.

Nick pulled out his notebook and pen and then pulled his rickety chair closer to the table.

Ruth looked at Bethan who seemed to be trying to avoid eye contact with both of them. 'We just wanted to ask you a few more questions about Aaron, if that's okay?'

Bethan shrugged defensively. 'Okay, but I didn't know him that well. He just came into the pub, that's all.'

Ruth could instantly see that she was lying to them – and she wasn't very good at it. She didn't blame her. She had been having an affair with an older married man. It wasn't something that she probably wanted to admit – especially to police officers.

'Could you tell us the nature of your relationship with Aaron?' Ruth asked.

'Relationship?' Bethan tried to compose herself. She visibly took a breath. 'I don't know what you mean.'

Nick's eyes searched her face. 'Were you and Aaron friends?'

She shrugged again and then began to bite at the cuticles on the nails of her right hand. 'I don't know. I suppose so.'

Ruth probed further. 'But you weren't more than friends?'

Bethan pulled a face as if the thought appalled her. 'No.'

'You're sure about that, Bethan? Because we're running

a murder investigation and it's very serious if you don't tell us the truth. In fact it's a criminal offence.'

Silence.

Bethan's eyes roamed nervously around the room as she continued to bite at her nails. She was clearly panicking.

'It's okay, Bethan,' Ruth said in a soft reassuring tone. 'We're not here to judge you. We just need to know everything about Aaron's life. And if you and Aaron were having a relationship then we need to know that. Just tell us the truth.'

Bethan looked away and then nodded.

Nick leaned forward. 'You and Aaron were having a relationship, is that right?'

Bethan nodded again but her eyes had now filled with tears.

'Can you tell us how long that had been going on?'

'A few months.' Bethan blew out her cheeks and wiped the tears away. 'But it had finished.'

Ruth furrowed her brow. 'Why did it finish?'

'His wife found out.'

'When did that happen?'

Bethan rubbed her face. 'About a week ago. I was devastated …'

Ruth shot a look at Nick. Natalie had made no mention of Aaron having an affair. Or the fact that she had just discovered this.

Chapter 28

Now wearing their blue forensic gloves, French and Kennedy had taken the weapons from the gun cabinet and laid them down very carefully on the kitchen table. Kennedy started to use her phone to take photos of the cabinet and the guns.

French began to inspect one of the semi-automatic machine guns. Something wasn't right. He'd noticed that they didn't weigh anywhere as much as he'd expected. Then he tapped at some gun components.

'That's weird,' he said with a confused expression. 'Some of this is made from plastic.' Then he inspected it further. 'In fact, quite a lot of it is plastic.'

'You mean it's a toy gun or a replica?' Kennedy asked.

'I don't think so.'

Kennedy came over looking confused. She inspected the gun carefully. 'That is very weird. I've never seen a gun with plastic parts before, but it looks very real to me.'

Then French remembered something he'd spotted in what looked like the dining room off the hallway.

'Hang on a second,' he said. 'Can you come with me?'

'Yeah.' She followed him out of the kitchen, down the hall and into the dining room.

There was a door on the far side.

French tried the door but it was locked.

He shrugged and then kicked the door hard with the sole of his shoe.

It crashed open.

On the other side was a tiny room that looked like a study.

Over by the window was a large PC and a laptop.

On a table, there was a black machine. It was about three foot high and had a rectangular frame. On top of the frame was a circular cylinder.

'Any idea what that is?' French asked as they went over to have a look.

'Yeah, it's a 3D printer.'

French pulled a face. 'Sorry. I've heard of them but I've no idea what they actually do.'

'Really?'

'Complete luddite,' he admitted. 'Guilty.'

Kennedy smiled. 'That machine creates little layers of plastic that all mould together. You link it to a computer. So, you can effectively 'print' a plastic plate, a cup or even toys. All sorts of stuff.'

French's eyes widened. 'What about gun parts?'

Kennedy shrugged. 'I've never heard of it but I guess you can actually manufacture anything.'

They shared a look.

'I guess we need ballistic forensics to have a look to see if those guns are viable?'

'They look pretty viable to me,' she said. 'Plus that cabinet is full of ammunition.'

'Jesus,' French muttered under his breath. 'Looks like Bellamy was manufacturing guns in this house. No wonder he did a runner when we turned up yesterday.'

'Yeah … I suppose you can order some of the metallic parts from abroad without raising too much suspicion. Then you build the rest on that machine. And hey presto, you've got a bloody machine gun.'

French shook his head. 'Doesn't bear thinking about.' Then he spotted something under the table. It was a black steel box about five feet long.

Crouching down, he pulled the box out and noticed that it was locked with a small padlock.

'Could have done with that crowbar,' he groaned. The uniformed officers had been called away on 'a shout' fifteen minutes earlier.

'A shout' was police slang for the report of an incident, usually over the phone or a police radio.

'We don't need a bloody crowbar,' Kennedy scoffed. 'Out the way, sarge.'

'Erm, okay …' French moved away as Kennedy came over and with an almighty stamp of her foot broke the padlock and the lock to the metal box.

She smiled with satisfaction. 'There we go. You're not the only one who can kick things open.'

French grinned. 'Fair point, well made.'

She gave him a knowing look as he reached over and flipped open the lid to the box.

Inside were rows and rows of plastic gun components.

There were also documents which he grabbed and started to look through.

Then he looked at Kennedy. 'These are plans of how to build a Skorpion submachine gun.'

'Which is the gun that Aaron Jenkins showed his brother and said that he was keeping for some 'very dangerous' people.'

Chapter 29

Ruth and Nick were making their way from Bethan Jones'
home and back out towards Manor Farm. They wanted to
know why Natalie had failed to tell them that she had
discovered that Aaron and Bethan were having an affair.
Ruth thought it was peculiar, as such a discovery would
have allowed Natalie to justify her relationship with
Charlie Jenkins in some way. Why hadn't she told them? It
was as if Natalie was hiding something else from them.

'Penny for them,' Nick said after a few minutes of
silence.

Ruth gave him a self-effacing smile. 'You can hear my
cogs whirring?'

'Actually it was the smoke coming out of your ears that
gave it away,' he joked.

Ruth gave a little laugh but her mind was still trying to
process all that they'd found out that day.

'My instinct is that Aaron was in contact with some
very moody people, possibly from Merseyside. And that for
some reason, he was holding on to a Skorpion submachine
gun for them,' Ruth said, thinking out loud.

'A gun that he was probably killed with,' Nick added.

'Indeed.'

'I sense that there's a 'but' coming,' Nick said, prompting her.

'I've always worked on the high probability in a murder case that the killer will be a partner, relative or someone very close to home. Aaron's wife was having an affair with his brother. But she also knew that he was sleeping with a local barmaid. As a tangled web of deceit and betrayal, it's the perfect set of circumstances for a murder.'

Nick raised an eyebrow. 'Basically you're saying that there are two lines of enquiry and, at this stage, you can't tell which one is the front runner. Which is unusual.'

'I couldn't have put it better if I'd tried,' Ruth admitted. She then gave him a bemused smile. 'You really do know me very well.'

Nick shrugged. 'We've been through a lot.'

'Ain't that the truth,' she joked as they took the turning to Manor Farm.

The track led downhill and the car bumped and banged as they hit various potholes along the way.

The sky was a sheet of pure blue and there wasn't a cloud to be seen. The only movement was the odd black or red grouse. Above them was a solitary peregrine falcon that was gliding gracefully on the warm air currents and looking down into the fields for prey.

With the views across the Vale of Llangollen to the Berwyn Mountains, they could have been somewhere in the Mediterranean. The valley itself was long and wide, with gentle slopes of green pasture broken only by dark hedgerows and dry stone walls.

Nick parked the car next to Natalie's red Mini Clubman that they'd seen before, so they knew she was inside. There had also been a call to say that the young constable who was acting as the FLO had been called away to give evidence at a trial in Chester and would be replaced by another constable the following morning.

Ruth walked up to the door and knocked.

There was silence except for a warm breeze that swept through nearby trees.

Ruth gave Nick a frown and then knocked again.

Nothing.

'Maybe she's out the back,' he suggested.

Ruth nodded. It was a beautiful afternoon to be stuck indoors.

They wandered around to the rear of the farmhouse where there was some dark grey rattan furniture and a folded garden umbrella with a rusty stand.

But there was no sign of Natalie.

Nick went to the back door and tried the handle but it was locked.

'You think she went for a walk?' Ruth wondered.

'Maybe,' Nick replied as he went to one of the ground floor windows. He cupped his hands so that he could see inside. 'I can't see anyone in the kitchen.'

For some reason, Ruth started to get an uneasy feeling about Natalie not being at home.

She pulled out her phone and rang the number that Natalie had given her. It went straight to voicemail.

'No answer. What about in there?' Ruth suggested, pointing to another ground floor window.

Nick nodded, went over, and squinted as he peered inside.

Then he immediately gave Ruth a serious look. 'Yeah, we need to go inside right now,' he said in an urgent tone.

'Is it Natalie?' she asked as they went to the back door.

He grabbed a stone from a nearby rockery. He shook

his head. 'No. I'm not sure, but something is definitely wrong.'

Taking the rock, he smashed the glass on the back door, reached inside and turned the key. Then he opened the door, and they went into the kitchen.

'This way,' he said, taking the lead.

As they went into the living room, Ruth instantly saw that the room had been turned upside down as if there had been a struggle.

'Shit,' she muttered under her breath. Whatever had happened, the room was an utter mess.

'Natalie?' Nick yelled. 'Natalie? It's the police.'

Going out into the hallway, Ruth stopped at the doorway to a small dining room.

'Natalie?' she shouted.

Then she spotted something. There were smears of blood on the white, painted door frame.

'Nick?' she said as she entered.

Inside the dining room there was a wooden chair with arms. It seemed out of place, as if it had been plonked in the middle of the carpet.

Nick came in and frowned. 'This doesn't look good.'

And then Ruth saw that there were two black plastic ties hanging off the arms of the chair.

'Someone has been tied to this chair,' she said, grabbing forensic gloves and putting them on.

'Natalie? Natalie? If you're here, you need to let us know!' Nick yelled.

They both listened, but there was just an eerie silence.

'I'll try upstairs,' Nick said as he jogged away.

Crouching down beside the chair, Ruth could see that there were small drips of blood on the green carpet. They seemed to be splattered all around the chair.

Looking closely at the dark oak chair, she could also see blood stains smeared on the wood.

Then out of the corner of her eye, she spotted something small and white in the fibres of the carpet.

'Nothing upstairs,' Nick sighed. He was slightly out of breath from searching the house for Natalie. 'And I've searched the ground floor again.'

Ruth held up the object she'd found on the carpet. 'I found a tooth,' she said to him with a grim expression.

'Jesus.' Nick shook his head.

Ruth took a clear evidence bag from her pocket and popped the tooth inside.

'Someone has been tied to this chair and been badly beaten,' Nick said quietly.

Ruth looked at him. 'And given that Natalie is missing, I think it's very likely to be her.'

Nick nodded in agreement.

Chapter 30

It was early evening as Ruth gathered the members of the CID team together. She had called Garrow who had reassured her that he would be back in CID the following morning. She knew that the CPS dropping charges against Lucy Morgan would have really got to him – but that was a conversation for the morning. She now had a murder and an abduction to deal with.

'Just to bring everyone up to speed,' she said, as she twisted the cap from a cold bottle of water. It might have been nearly 8pm but the evening was still very warm. 'As most of you know, we believe that Natalie Jenkins has been abducted from her home at some point this afternoon. There were signs of a struggle and also signs that she may have been tied up, attacked, or even tortured.' Ruth then gestured over to French and Kennedy. 'From what you guys found at Ian Bellamy's home, it's clear that there is some kind of illegal firearms manufacturing going on. We know that Aaron met with Bellamy at The Red Lion pub at lunchtime only a couple of hours before he was shot dead. And we know that he was killed with a submachine gun, possibly the Skorpion gun that he told his brother he was keeping for what he termed 'dangerous people'.'

French looked over. 'And that also fits in with the guns and plans that we found at Bellamy's home. They are all for a Skorpion submachine gun.'

Kennedy's phone rang and she moved away to take the call.

Nick nodded. 'And we know that Aaron had met with some very dubious looking characters from Merseyside.'

Ruth glanced over at Georgie. 'Any news on the registration of that Range Rover we saw in the car park?'

'I ran it through with the DVLA,' she said. 'They told me that the plate had been reported stolen six months ago.'

'Great,' Ruth sighed. It wasn't a huge surprise. Men like that knew exactly how to cover their tracks.

Kennedy came back over and gestured to her phone. 'Boss, I put out some feelers to a contact I've got in the NCA.'

The NCA – National Crime Agency – was a national law enforcement unit for the whole of the UK. They focussed on organised crime, especially weapon and drugs trafficking.

'What did they have to say?' Ruth asked.

Kennedy gave them all a significant look. 'Seems that they're running a joint operation with Merseyside Police Organised Crime Task Force. And they have suspects in firearms trafficking that they think they can link to the Llangollen area.'

Ruth's eyes widened. It seemed that they had uncovered something more significant than they had expected.

'They want the SIO or deputy SIO to call them asap.'

Ruth signalled to Nick that she wanted him to do it.

'Good. Thanks Jade. Right, great work today everyone.

I don't want to see anyone here after eleven tonight. Back in by six tomorrow morning, except for the night shift.'

Ruth began to walk towards her office, noticing how drained she felt. Maybe she was too old to keep doing this?

'Boss,' Georgie called over. She was holding her phone.

'Yes?' Ruth asked with an enquiring look.

'Call from a uniformed patrol. They've found a body in the woods at Nant Mill and they think it's Natalie Jenkins.'

Chapter 31

Ruth and Nick were speeding down the A483 towards Nant Mill and the nearby woods. The sun had nearly set and the horizon was awash with burned orange and dark pink. It was stunning.

'I'm still trying to put all this together,' Ruth admitted as she reached for a cigarette. Smoking helped her think. Or at least that was her excuse and she was sticking to it.

'I guess we're thinking that whoever Aaron was holding that gun for turned up at Manor Farm on Monday afternoon,' Nick stated.

'And given what the NCA said, these people might be from Merseyside. Possibly the men we saw on the CCTV at The Red Lion pub.'

'Exactly. And then something went horribly wrong and they decided to shoot Aaron.'

'Maybe he'd been shooting his mouth off to the wrong people about having the gun in his possession,' Ruth suggested. 'If you remember, Charlie Jenkins told us that Aaron got drunk, got out the Skorpion and was showing off about having it.'

'Yeah, maybe they were pissed off that he had been bragging,' Nick said, 'and they just turned up to get their gun back and shut Aaron up for good.'

He clicked the indicator as they took the turning for Nant Mill Wood.

'How does Ian Bellamy and his plastic guns fit into all this?' he asked.

'I'm not sure. Maybe Bellamy was manufacturing guns for whoever the Task Force are looking at and Aaron was helping him.'

As Ruth looked up, she saw that two marked patrol cars with their blue lights flashing had pulled across the top of the steep road down to Nant Mill.

Nick pulled the car over and parked.

'Why did they come back, torture, abduct and then kill Natalie?' Nick wondered out loud.

'Maybe she knew too much,' Ruth suggested. 'They didn't want to take a chance that now Aaron was dead, she wouldn't go to the police with what she knew about the firearms.'

'Sounds about right,' Nick agreed.

They began to make their way down the steep road to the Nant Mill Visitors' Centre. The air was still warm and smelled of the nearby woodlands which consisted of conifers, as well as beech, ash and oak. There was also the sweet scent of the polypody fern mixed with wild garlic.

In the car park, the SOCO van was parked up and its back doors were open. Several forensic officers in white nitrile suits were over by an area of tall grasses and scrubs about thirty yards from the car park and under some oak trees.

A middle-aged uniformed male police officer in a high vis jacket gave them a quizzical look as they approached.

In fact he looked like he was about to ask them what they were doing and tell them to turn around.

Ruth and Nick pulled out their warrant cards. 'DI Hunter and DS Evans, Llancastell CID,' Ruth explained.

'Right you are, ma'am,' he said, as if he'd known exactly who they were all along.

'What have we got, constable?' Ruth asked.

'Victim is a Natalie Jenkins. We found a credit card in her trouser pocket.'

Ruth's heart sank. It seemed that Natalie was just an innocent woman who had got caught up in her husband's criminal activity.

'Cause of death?'

'She's been shot in the head.' The constable then lowered his voice. 'Between the eyes. I'm no expert but whoever did this knew what they were doing.'

'Who discovered her?'

'Dog walker. He let his Lab off the lead and he went straight over to the victim.' He pointed to where the SOCOs were standing and crouching under the trees. The light dappled through the leaves giving the scene a slightly ghostly appearance.

'Where is he now?' Ruth enquired.

The constable gestured to a man in his 30s who was sitting on a dry stone wall with a black Labrador at his feet. He was vaping and looked lost in thought.

'That's him over there, ma'am. He's very shaken.' He looked down at his notepad. 'Huw Ramsey. He says he comes here every day at this time.'

'Did he see anything or anyone significant?' Nick asked.

The constable shook his head. 'He said there were a few kids on their bikes but they disappeared.'

'But nothing suspicious?' Nick said to clarify.

'Apparently not.' The constable shrugged. 'She wouldn't have been there for long. Whoever killed her didn't do much to hide where she was. It's as if they took her over there, shot her in the head and then left. Brutal. I've been on the job over twenty years and I've never seen anything like it.'

Ruth didn't like to say that in the thirty years she'd been on the job she'd seen more than her fair share of cold-blooded murders and shootings.

'Okay, thank you, constable,' she said, giving him a reassuring look.

Nick pointed over at the building which housed the Nant Mill Visitors' Centre. 'Don't suppose they've got CCTV anywhere around here?'

The constable shook his head slowly. 'I've asked the woman inside, but she says they haven't.'

Nick nodded his acknowledgement as he and Ruth turned and began to make their way over to where the SOCOs were gathered.

'Sounds like a professional hit,' Nick said under his breath.

'Which would fit if we think that Natalie was taken by whoever Aaron and Bellamy were dealing with.'

A figure in a white forensic suit, mask, hat and rubber boots approached.

Before they said anything, Ruth knew who it was.

Professor Tony Amis.

Amis had a slightly odd walk. He took short deliberate steps as if he was uncertain of his balance. It made him look a little bit like a penguin walking along.

'Hello, Tony,' Ruth said.

'Ah, here they are,' Amis said in his usual jovial tone. Then he turned to look back at the body that Ruth and Nick could now see lying in the grass. 'Natalie Jenkins.

I'm assuming she is the wife of your victim from Monday?'

'Correct,' Nick replied.

'Gunshot to the head, is that right?' Ruth enquired.

'Yep,' Amis said, pulling down his mask. 'Execution style. Very cold.' Then he blew out his ruddy cheeks. 'It's way too hot to be prancing around in one of these forensic suits. And don't even get me going on these bloody boots.' Then he looked at them. 'You know the best place to be on a day like today?'

Ruth was already one step ahead of him. She gave him a withering look. 'Please don't say a mortuary, Tony,' she groaned.

'Okay,' he shrugged, 'but on a boiling day like today, there's no place like it.'

'Apart from all the dead bodies,' Nick joked dryly.

'They don't bother me. Never have done actually. They're dead. They're not going anywhere and they're not going to say anything. Perfect companions if you think about it.'

Ruth looked at him and then rolled her eyes.

'Anything else you can tell us at this stage?' she asked, trying not to show her impatience.

'Your victim was badly beaten.'

Ruth nodded. 'We think she was tied to a chair. We found blood and a tooth at her home.'

Amis gave them a dark look. 'Whoever did this to her is very cold and very dangerous.'

Chapter 32

Ruth stood looking up at the scene board. A photo of Natalie had been pinned up close to Aaron's. For a few seconds, she reflected on Natalie's violent death. Even after all these years as a serving police officer, it was difficult when someone like Natalie got caught up in something so violent. After all, she was an innocent primary school teacher who had clearly dedicated her life to helping children. It was terrible to think that she had somehow got caught up in the world of Aaron and Bellamy's construction and trafficking of illegal firearms to organised criminals. And that had resulted in her brutal torture and cold-blooded murder.

Georgie approached looking at a printout. 'Boss, we've got a possible eyewitness from this afternoon.'

'Go on,' Ruth said, trying to refocus.

'A woman said she was running along the road,' Georgie said as she then consulted her notes. 'Abbey Road, which is the A542. It's the road that the track to Manor Farm is off.'

'Yeah, I know it.'

'She saw a black Range Rover pulling out of the turning to Manor Farm at speed. In fact, they nearly ran her over.'

'I don't suppose she saw the registration?' Ruth asked hopefully.

Georgie shook her head. 'No. But she did say that the windows were tinted so she couldn't see inside.'

'Sounds like the same vehicle that we saw on the CCTV at The Red Lion,' Ruth stated, thinking out loud.

'That's what I thought, boss.'

'Does she know what time it was?'

'About 4pm, she thinks.'

'Thank you, Georgie.' If the eyewitness was correct, Natalie Jenkins was dead three hours later.

As Ruth turned away from the scene board and headed back towards her office she spotted Nick sitting on his desk, drinking coffee. His tie was loosened – it had been a long hot day.

'I've spoken to the NCA,' he said.

'Any joy?'

'Yeah. Something to do with an Operation Venus that they're running in conjunction with the Merseyside Police Organised Crime Task Force. I spoke to a DS Sophie Kent. They're going to come here first thing tomorrow to brief us and find out what we've come up with.'

'Great stuff,' Ruth said with a positive nod. It was progress that the NCA had confirmed an interest in what Nick had told them. It meant that they were on the right track.

'Boss?' French called over.

Ruth went over to French's desk where he was sitting in front of a computer screen. 'What is it?'

'I pulled all Aaron Jenkins' bank accounts. He had an

account for the farm which was run as a limited company, and then a joint bank account with Natalie.'

'What did you find?'

'There's nothing suspicious in either of the accounts, but it does show that Manor Farm was losing money hand over fist.'

'Which explains why they were on the verge of bankruptcy.'

'Yeah, but Aaron also had another bank account with a different bank. It's a business account in the name of Jenkins Holdings Ltd.'

'What does it do?'

'According to Companies House it's an import and export company dealing with machine parts.'

Ruth's instinct was that the 'machine parts' that Aaron Jenkins was importing were in fact components for firearms.

'And the other strange thing is that there is £125,000 sitting in that account,' French said, pointing to the screen.

'So, Aaron Jenkins wasn't skint at all?'

'No, boss, and there are several large payments from PTC Security in the account.'

'Which implies that Gary Williams might be involved too,' Ruth said. Everything was now starting to piece together.

French looked at her. 'Maybe Aaron had found a far more lucrative business than farming.'

'Sounds like he was going to let the farm go bankrupt and concentrate on manufacturing and selling firearms. Except somewhere along the line it went horribly wrong.'

Chapter 33

It was 6am the next morning as Ruth stood quietly in the canteen at Llancastell nick. She was lost in thought. In fact she was juggling various things that were preoccupying her. The ongoing quest to adopt Daniel weighed heavily on her shoulders. Every day that went by, she, Sarah and Daniel seemed to become a more settled, comfortable family unit. Clearly it wasn't a usual or 'normal' family unit. But it was 2021. The term 'blended family' was now used for anything outside of the traditional parameters of the nuclear family. In fact in the old days the term '2.4 kids' was often used to mean an average family, as that was the 'average' number of children a UK family had. It had even spawned a 90s UK sitcom of that name.

Ruth was also worried about DC Jim Garrow. Having heard that the preliminary hearing in the case against Lucy Morgan had collapsed, she suspected that his close relationship with Lucy after her mother's murder had been used to discredit his evidence. Garrow had called in sick yesterday which was unheard of. If he didn't turn up for work this morning, she promised herself she would pop round to see him on her way home from work. Like most of the younger members of the Llancastell CID team, Ruth felt a little maternal towards Garrow. She remembered when she'd first met him a few years earlier. He was still in uniform when he'd got caught up in an incident at an MI5 safehouse with a suspected Islamic terrorist. He had handled himself incredibly well in very difficult circumstances, and Ruth had been impressed by him as an officer ever since.

'Are you buying a coffee or shall I push in front of you?' asked a voice.

For a second, Ruth was going to react, but then realised she recognised the voice and the sarcastic tone.

It was Nick.

'Very funny,' she said, rolling her eyes.

They had come into the station at the crack of dawn to meet with officers from Merseyside Police Organised Crime Task Force. Ruth had dealt with officers from this unit before and always found them to be easy to work with – which was a relief. Her recent dealings with Cheshire Police had been challenging and problematic.

'How are things back at the ranch?' Ruth asked as she took a mug, placed it under the coffee machine and pressed the 'Latte' button.

'We're all fine,' Nick replied unconvincingly.

Ruth took her mug from the machine. 'Yeah, well I don't believe that for one second.'

Nick took a mug and popped it under the coffee machine. 'Amanda wants another child.'

'I think you've told me that before haven't you?'

'We were talking about it,' he said as he took his mug of coffee from the machine, 'but now we're just going ahead.'

'You sound delighted about that,' Ruth quipped dryly.

'I'd love to have another kid. And it would be great for Megan, but Amanda seems to think that it has to happen right now and that we're running out of time.'

'Just be patient with her. Trying to conceive can feel stressful, especially if it doesn't happen straight away.'

'It happened straight away last time,' he stated.

'That was an accident, you dope.'

Nick looked baffled. 'So what?'

'You weren't trying. There was no pressure. As soon as there's pressure, things stop working.'

'Not my end, they don't.'

Ruth gave him a withering look as they moved towards the till and she used her card to pay for both coffees.

'Firstly, ewww. That's too much information, thank you,' she groaned. 'And secondly, you've got the easy bit. A few minutes and bang, job done.'

'A few minutes?' he protested with a grin.

Ruth laughed. 'Jesus, Nick, what is wrong with you this morning?'

He sighed with a self-effacing smile. 'I don't know. I'm tired, I guess.'

As they headed towards the canteen exit, Ruth glanced at her watch. 'We'd better go and meet our guests from over the border.'

Chapter 34

Five minutes later, Ruth and Nick arrived at the main meeting room on the ground floor. Ruth could see that the two officers from Merseyside had already arrived and were chatting and drinking coffee.

Opening the door, she gave them both a friendly smile.

A woman in her 40s, short dark hair, piercing blue eyes, and wearing a smart trouser suit got up and approached.

'DS Sophie Kent,' she said, introducing herself and shaking their hands firmly.

'Pleased to meet you. I'm DI Ruth Hunter. This is DS Nick Evans.'

'And this is my colleague, DC Amit Popat.'

DC Popat was in his 20s, slim, Asian, with black hair cut into a fashionable quiff. He was wearing a smart navy suit.

There were more handshakes, and Ruth and Nick sat down on the opposite side of the meeting table.

'Thanks for coming over to see us,' Ruth said.

Kent looked over. 'We thought it better for us to do this face to face.'

Popat shifted forward on his seat. He had some folders on the table in front of him. 'We understand that you've got two murders that you believe are connected to the manufacture and possible trafficking of firearms. And that you think there's a connection to Merseyside?'

Ruth nodded to confirm that what he said was spot on. She grabbed a folder, pulled it over and then took out a photograph.

'This is Aaron Jenkins. He's ex-military. Served with the Welsh Guards in Afghanistan just over ten years ago. On Monday afternoon he was shot dead with a submachine gun in a field on his farm.'

Nick took another photo and pointed to it. 'Inside Aaron's home we found this empty gun cabinet along with this box of 9mm ammunition. Aaron had told his brother Charlie, who is also ex-military, that he was holding a submachine gun for some 'very dangerous' people. He showed him a Skorpion EVO 3 firearm.'

Kent and Popat glanced at each other.

Ruth pulled out another photograph and turned it to show them. 'On the day he was murdered, Aaron met this man, Ian Bellamy. They had served together in Afghanistan. When we attempted to question Bellamy about this meeting he tried to evade us, crashed his vehicle, and is now in the ICU in a coma at Llancastell University Hospital.' Ruth pulled out two more photos to show. 'My officers searched Bellamy's home. In a locked gun cabinet they found six more Skorpion EVO 3 firearms and ammunition.'

'Jesus,' Kent said under her breath.

Ruth wasn't surprised by Kent's reaction. The devastation that half a dozen submachine guns could do on the streets of Liverpool was unthinkable.

Nick raised an eyebrow. 'The strange thing is, a lot of

the body and components of these guns were made from plastic. Some of the trigger mechanisms, chambers, and firing pins were made from metal.'

Kent and Popat nodded as if they weren't hugely surprised by this.

Ruth showed them another photo. 'Then we found this 3D printer along with a box of plastic gun components.' Ruth gave them a dark look. 'Natalie Jenkins, Aaron's wife, was tortured at her home yesterday. Then she was abducted, shot in the head, and dumped.'

'Yes, we saw that on the news,' Kent said with a serious expression.

Nick took his laptop, opened it, and then turned the screen to show Kent and Popat. He clicked a button and the CCTV from The Red Lion car park flashed up on the screen.

'A few weeks ago, the two men from this Range Rover met with Aaron at The Red Lion pub.' Nick pointed to the moving image of the two men parking and getting out of the car. 'They had Merseyside accents. We've run the registration but according to the DVLA the plates are stolen. The same car was spotted yesterday afternoon leaving Manor Farm. We assume that this is when Natalie Jenkins was abducted.'

Kent leaned forward and peered closely at the CCTV footage. 'Connor Bradley and Shaun Peterson,' she said, giving Popat a knowing look.

Nick narrowed his eyes. 'You obviously know these guys?'

'Yes,' Popat said. 'We've had them under obs all year. They're part of an OCG based in Birkenhead and Rock Ferry on The Wirral.'

'And I assume they deal in firearms?' Ruth asked.

'Mainly,' Kent replied. 'Some drug dealing along the

North Wales coast. But they supply guns to gangs in Liverpool and are well known for it. Or at least they used to supply guns.'

Ruth then remembered the BBC News story she'd seen recently about a shipment of firearms being seized at Liverpool Docks. 'I saw you intercepted a cargo of guns a few days ago?'

'That's right,' Popat confirmed. 'Our biggest haul yet. And it's the third one this year.'

Ruth furrowed her brow. 'You didn't seem surprised when we mentioned the 3D printer and the plastic parts for the guns that we discovered?'

Kent shook her head. 'We're just starting to see these guns on the market,' she explained.

'I guess it's a result of our seizures of firearms at the port,' Popat said. 'Gangs are looking at different ways of creating guns because there are so few in circulation.'

'We're seeing replica guns being converted to live firearms,' Kent added, 'and now we're starting to come across the 3D printer manufacture of gun parts or even 90% of a firearm.'

'Did you know that these guys from Birkenhead had come across the border?' Ruth enquired.

'Yes,' said Popat, 'we'd tracked them coming over to North Wales a few times but we didn't know what they were up to.'

Kent gave them a knowing look. 'But now we do.'

Nick scratched his beard and sat back in his chair. 'The only thing is, we have no idea why Aaron or Natalie were murdered yet.'

'Deal gone wrong?' Kent suggested.

'Maybe,' Ruth said. 'We believe that the Skorpion gun Aaron kept in his gun cabinet was the firearm that was used to kill him. I've asked forensic ballistics to take a look. But it does mean that the gun from the farm is missing.'

'If Bradley and Peterson shot and killed Aaron,' Popat said, 'they would have taken that gun with them.'

Nick leaned forward and placed his forearms on the table. 'That doesn't add up though does it?'

Kent gave him a quizzical look. 'Why not?'

'If Bradley and Peterson murdered Aaron Jenkins because they were either double-crossing him or he was holding out on them on payment, why would they risk coming back, torturing, abducting and then killing Natalie? It doesn't make any sense.'

'Clearly they thought Natalie Jenkins had information that they wanted to get out of her,' Popat said. 'When she refused, or couldn't provide adequate answers, they took her and killed her.'

Then Ruth had a dark thought. 'And maybe Bradley and Peterson are getting rid of anyone this side of the border that they've been dealing with.'

Nick turned his head to look at her. 'Ian Bellamy?'

There were a few seconds of silence.

Kent nodded. 'Yeah, he could be in significant danger if Bradley and Peterson think there's any chance that he will talk.'

Ruth felt uneasy. 'I'll get an authorised firearms officer over to Bellamy's hospital room as soon as possible.'

Chapter 35

Ruth had just finished her call to arrange an AFO to travel to the University Hospital in Llancastell to guard Bellamy. Bradley and Peterson had shown themselves to be cold-blooded, callous killers, so walking into the hospital and shooting Bellamy dead as a safety precaution definitely wasn't beyond them. And the thought of that happening on her watch made Ruth shudder.

A figure appeared at the door and gave it a knock.

It was Garrow.

Ruth gestured for him to come in and sit down. 'Hey, aren't you a sight for sore eyes, Jim?'

'I'm surprised they let me in the building,' he said with an uncomfortable shrug.

'Don't be silly.' Ruth could see how tired and drawn he looked.

Out of the corner of her eye, she spotted Georgie walking across the CID office holding a huge bunch of flowers. As far as Ruth knew, Georgie didn't have any male admirers so she wondered who they were for.

Garrow gave an audible sigh. The stress of the

hearing had clearly got to him. But he was one of the good guys. He worked hard and kept his nose clean, but he had made the mistake of getting too close to a witness.

Ruth met his gaze. She sensed that he was keeping something from her.

'What is it?' she asked, to prompt him.

'She came to my house,' he said quietly.

'What?' Ruth didn't like the sound of that one bit. 'Lucy Morgan?'

'Yes.'

'Explain.'

He took a deep breath. 'The night before last. She knocked on the door. And then she got into my back garden and came up to my patio doors to look in at me. And then she laughed and disappeared.'

Ruth sighed under her breath. 'Jesus, Jim.' Despite the case against Lucy Morgan being dropped, Ruth had seen the evidence. Lucy had faked amnesia after slitting her mother's throat in a fit of rage. That meant she was incredibly dangerous, especially if she was now obsessed with making Garrow's life hell.

'I don't want any fuss,' he admitted. 'I feel guilty enough as it is.'

'Nonsense,' Ruth said forcefully. 'We need to get a restraining order on her for starters. And some form of protection for you.'

Garrow shook his head. 'I can't have officers wasting their time protecting me.'

Ruth looked at him. 'You're one of the best officers in this CID team.'

Before she could continue, Georgie arrived with the bunch of flowers.

'Aw, Georgie, you shouldn't have,' Ruth joked, although

she did wonder why Georgie was still walking around with the flowers.

Georgie turned to Garrow. 'There you are. I've been looking for you everywhere.' Then she winked at Ruth. 'These are for Jim.'

'Really?' Garrow looked baffled.

For a second, Ruth gave an amused smile and looked at Georgie. 'Did we get the details of Aaron Jenkins' will back from his solicitor yet?'

'Due this afternoon,' she replied, and then she turned to Garrow. 'I'll leave you to it then Jim,' she said with a smirk.

Then a dark thought came to Ruth as Garrow pulled out the card attached to the flowers.

His face fell when he read it.

Ruth gestured for him to hand the card over. She was already one step ahead of him.

JIM,
You know I will always love you. Just
let me know when you're ready.
Don't push me away.
Love, Lucy xxx

RUTH LET OUT A CONCERNED SIGH. Then she looked directly at him. 'This isn't good. And as far as I can see, she isn't going away any time soon, is she?'

Garrow shook his head frustratedly. 'No, boss. I'm sorry.'

'You're not responsible for Lucy Morgan being a psychopath so stop being so bloody apologetic,' Ruth said in a firm tone. 'And you will be getting uniformed patrols coming past your home to keep a check. If anything else happens, then I'll be posting an officer at your home permanently.'

'Okay, boss. And thank you.'

Before they could continue, Nick knocked on her open door.

Ruth looked up at him.

'The AFO is going to be at the hospital in fifteen minutes. I thought we should go and brief him?' Nick suggested.

'Of course,' Ruth said, getting up from her chair.

Nick gave Garrow a quizzical look. 'Flowers? Who's the lucky girl?'

Garrow got to his feet and groaned under his breath. 'Don't ask.'

Ruth gave Nick a forced smile. 'I'll explain in the car.'

'Professor Amis is doing the preliminary post-mortem on Natalie Jenkins,' Nick said. 'He'd like us to pop in as there's something he'd like to show us.'

Ruth sighed. 'There usually is, but we're going to the hospital so we can kill two birds with one stone, if you'll excuse the horrible pun.'

Chapter 36

Ruth and Nick marched along the corridor of the second floor of the hospital towards the Intensive Care Unit. Ruth hadn't been back there since she had been shot and nearly died earlier in the year. It was the smell of hospital food mixed with detergents and cleaning fluids that brought back those memories.

The sight of the sign for the ICU suddenly made her feel a bit unsteady. She slowed down a little. Up until this point, she hadn't given going back to the hospital a second thought. She certainly didn't think that it would trigger any emotional response. After all, since she'd arrived in North Wales she'd been to the hospital and its ICU dozens of times. However, clearly the trauma of being shot and having a cardiac arrest had affected her more than she realised. She had been offered some counselling by the North Wales Police after the incident and she'd had six counselling sessions with a lovely psychotherapist called Nicola. After that, she had been confident that what had happened was now water under the bridge.

'You okay?' Nick asked, looking a little concerned.

'Yeah,' Ruth replied as she took a breath to steady herself. 'I'll be fine.' But her heart was hammering away in her chest as if she'd sprinted for a bus. She started to take some long, deep breaths.

Putting his hand on her shoulder, Nick led her over to some seats against the wall in the corridor.

The breathing seemed to ease what Ruth knew to be a panic attack. She'd done breathing exercises in the past to deal with anxiety.

'It's okay,' he said quietly, 'take your time.'

Ruth could feel her heart had started to slow as she continued to breathe deeply. 'That's better,' she said quietly as she slowly nodded her head.

'Why don't you stay here while I brief the AFO?' Nick suggested.

Ruth shook her head. 'I'm fine,' she reassured him. 'Honestly. I just needed to get my breath.'

Blowing out her cheeks, she stood up and was relieved that the dizziness had gone and her head was now clear. Whatever had happened, it had passed.

For now.

She nudged Nick's arm. 'Don't worry. Come on, we need to speak to the AFO. Do we have a name yet?'

Nick took out his phone and glanced down at the screen. 'Sergeant Eamon O'Hara,' he said, reading the name of the AFO.

'Sounds Russian,' Ruth joked.

'Very good.' Nick laughed. 'He's come up from St Asaph.'

It had been a few years since the armed police units of both North Wales and Cheshire merged due to budget cuts. They had formed the AAPU - the Alliance Armed

Policing Unit. One of the main headquarters for this unit was the city of St Asaph.

As they arrived at the corridor of the ICU, they spotted a man in his 30s. He was dressed in a black police uniform and had a Glock 17 handgun in a holster on his hip.

'Sergeant O'Hara?' Ruth asked, as she and Nick pulled out their warrant cards.

'Yes,' he said with a serious expression. He had coal-black hair and beard and dark skin.

'DI Hunter and DS Evans, Llancastell CID. I spoke to a Chief Inspector Morley earlier today.'

'Yes, ma'am.'

'And he explained why you're here?'

O'Hara nodded. 'He told me the basics.'

Ruth gestured to a small row of empty seats against the wall. 'Take a pew and we'll fill in the blanks.'

Sitting down, Nick reached into a folder that he'd been carrying. Inside was a document that had two photographs printed on it with two names underneath. Connor Bradley and Shaun Peterson.

He handed the document to O'Hara. 'These two men are Connor Bradley and Shaun Peterson. They are part of a criminal gang based in Birkenhead on The Wirral who source and traffick firearms into Liverpool.'

'Yes,' O'Hara said as he took the document and studied the photographs.

Ruth gestured to the white doors of the ICU. 'The man you're protecting is Ian Bellamy. We believe that Bellamy was manufacturing guns for Bradley and Peterson. However, something along the way has gone wrong and ...' Ruth pointed to the document O'Hara was holding, '... these two men are trying to murder anyone involved before they talk to us.'

'Yes, ma'am,' O'Hara said.

Ruth fixed her eyes on his. 'Make no mistake, these two men are incredibly dangerous. They are cold-blooded killers.'

Chapter 37

French and Kennedy were on their way to the PTC Security compound where they had spoken to Gary Williams two days ago. Having found significant payments from PTC Security to Aaron Jenkins, it was clear that there was something incredibly suspicious going on. And putting two and two together, it wasn't a far stretch to believe that PTC Security was a front for the manufacture and trafficking of illegal firearms. It also meant that Gary Williams, the owner of PTC Security, had lied to them when they last visited. He knew full well why Ian Bellamy and Aaron Jenkins had met at The Red Lion pub on the day that Aaron was murdered. In fact, Gary might well be involved in Aaron's murder. They had no idea, but they had a warrant for his arrest and intended to take him back to Llancastell nick for questioning. They had also obtained a Section 18 Search Warrant for the premises that PTC Security owned.

There was also another major issue. Having made several phone calls, French had been unable to speak to anyone at PTC Security that day. That had made him feel uneasy. After Ruth and Nick's meeting with officers from the Merseyside Police Organised Crime Task Force, they knew how incredibly dangerous the OCG from Birkenhead was. If Connor Bradley and Shaun Peterson were attempting to 'silence' everyone who had been involved in the manufacture and trafficking of the Skorpion submachine guns, then Gary Williams, and possibly others at PTC Security, might well be on their hit list. They needed to be warned that their lives could be in great danger and to take appropriate precautions.

As they drove into Corwen, the traffic slowed to a halt for some temporary lights on the high street. The town was bustling, as Snowdonia was flooded with tourists at this time of the year. French looked out at a couple with two small children dressed in little sunhats and colourful sunglasses who were absorbed in eating ice creams. As the family went to cross the road in front of their car, the parents reached out for their children's hands and guided them safely across.

French sensed Kennedy looking over at him.

He turned and gave her a questioning look.

'Aw,' she said in a teasing tone as she gave him a warm smile.

'What?' he asked defensively.

'Cute aren't they?' she said, pointing at the kids. Then she looked back at him. 'You want kids?'

'Definitely,' he answered immediately.

'Right.' She paused for a moment. 'Anyone significant in your life?'

'Nah.' He chuckled, then pointed to his face. 'Not many takers with a face like this,' he joked, but he suddenly felt self-conscious.

Kennedy stared at him. 'What are you talking about?

At the risk of being inappropriate, you're a handsome man.'

French shook his head. 'Thanks, but I know that's not true.' No one had ever described him as handsome, not even his mother. At best he considered himself 'average'.

'And quite a catch for a lucky lady,' she said with a grin.

'Are you mocking me, DC Kennedy?'

'No,' she protested. 'Good job, own your own home, nice looking, not a total twat.'

French laughed. 'Not a total twat? Oh thanks.'

For a brief moment, they held each other's gaze as their eyes met. French didn't know if he was imagining it, but was there a little spark of attraction?

There was silence in the car for a short while.

Was that really awkward? French wondered as he looked out of the window.

Then over on the pavement, he saw something that caught his eye.

It was the larger than life-size bronze statue of Owain Glyndwr on his horse. He was wearing armour and holding a sword aloft in his right hand. It was set in a huge plinth of polished granite.

'My favourite statue in North Wales,' he said, with a gesturing nod of his head. He was glad to break the tension and change the subject matter.

'Pretty impressive.'

'You know who that is?'

Kennedy lowered her sunglasses to take a better look. 'Nope.'

'Owain Glyndwr,' French said proudly.

'Okay.'

French had a bemused expression. 'You don't know who Owain Glyndwr is, do you?'

'Nope. Should I?'

'Now that you're in North Wales, you definitely should. Owain Glyndwr is the last crowned Prince of Wales and a Welsh nationalist hero. He came from around here.'

'What did he do?'

'He fought against the English in the Welsh rebellion of the early 1400s,' French explained, 'and when the English conquered North Wales as far as Harlech, he went into hiding and was never captured. Legend has it that when the Welsh rise again, he will return to lead us.'

Kennedy smiled at him. 'I like that.'

French beamed back at her. Talking about Owain Glyndwr had aroused his Welsh national pride.

The traffic lights changed and they drove out of Corwen and on towards the PTC Security compound.

As they made their way up the dusty, bumpy track, French was still lost in their conversation and the possibility that there might be something between him and Kennedy. However, he then told himself to get his head back on the job and not get distracted. Getting distracted could be incredibly dangerous.

Pulling into the compound, French slowed and glanced around. It looked exactly the same as it had done two days earlier.

Then Kennedy's face fell and she pointed over to the far corner of the compound. French squinted. Almost hidden behind one of the buildings and the dark shadows cast by the tall trees that surrounded the area was a car.

A black Range Rover with tinted windows.

French then clocked the registration. It was the same car that had been identified as belonging to Connor Bradley and Shaun Peterson.

'Shit,' he said under his breath.

'Shit indeed,' Kennedy agreed.

Chapter 38

Ruth and Nick stood in the old metallic lift going down from the ground floor to the windowless basement of the hospital where the mortuary was located.

'Never got the fascination with guns,' Ruth commented.

Nick gave her an enquiring look as if to say that he didn't know what she meant.

'I mean in the police force. In the old days in CID in the Met, there were some officers who would wet themselves if they thought we were going to take firearms on an operation. They loved it.'

'Boys and their toys,' Nick joked.

'If I'm honest, guns scare the life out of me.'

'What did you have back in the day? The old Smith and Wesson .38 revolver?' he asked with a grin.

'You see?' Ruth rolled her eyes. 'You're just as bad.'

Nick gave an innocent shrug as the lift stopped at the basement with an unsettling metallic clunk, and the doors opened very slowly.

They walked down the sterile, windowless corridor

towards the double doors that led to the mortuary. Ruth knew that they would be met with the familiar routine by Professor Amis.

'How're you feeling now?' Nick asked as he gestured to the doors. 'Okay to go in here?'

Ruth was touched by Nick's concern, even if he was being a little over-protective.

'Thanks but I'm fine. Really,' she reassured him as they went inside.

The air inside the mortuary was nice and cool, even if it did smell of chemicals and preserving fluids.

Amis looked across the room at them. He had Aaron's body on one metal examining table. To the left of that, Natalie's body was laid out.

Ruth didn't think she'd ever been into a mortuary when two bodies had been laid out side by side. And certainly not a married couple. Whatever Amis wanted to show them, it was clear that it required them to see both victims.

Pulling down his mask, Ruth noticed that Amis now had bright, straight white teeth. In fact they were *very* white. She hadn't noticed them earlier in the week. Even though they were verging on fluorescent, they were a huge improvement on the yellowing, uneven set he'd had before. And being a chief pathologist, she was sure that he could afford them.

'I need you guys to come over and look at both your victims,' he explained as he gestured.

As he spoke, Ruth's eyes were immediately drawn to his mouth. She couldn't help it.

Amis noticed.

'Oh, my teeth?' he asked with his uber bright smile. He didn't seem remotely offended that she was staring at them.

'I think they look great,' she said in a positive tone.

'Yes, they do don't they?' Amis agreed in his booming, jovial voice.

Nick seemed to be hiding a smirk. 'In fact, if you don't mind me saying, a huge improvement.'

'I don't mind you saying that at all, young man,' Amis replied with a chortle. 'I think they call them Turkey Teeth these days, but I went up to Liverpool to get them done. Same dentist that all the footballers use. You know, Klopp, etc …' Then he paused. 'You don't think they're too much, do you? My wife thinks they're ridiculous.'

Ruth shook her head and wondered quite how they'd managed to get caught up in a long conversation about Amis' teeth while she had a double murder investigation to run.

'They look great, Tony,' Nick reassured him.

'Good, good.' Amis nodded and then blinked. 'Right, where were we?' Then he turned around and beckoned them over to the white bodies of Aaron and Natalie Jenkins.

Aaron's body already had all the hallmarks of a post-mortem. Thick stitches where his body had been opened to examine his organs and the various bullet wounds. Natalie's body still hadn't been fully examined or cut open.

Moving forward, Ruth could see the dark hole on Natalie's temple where she had been shot at close range. The skin around it was reddy black, which Ruth knew signified that she had been killed at very close range and received powder burns.

'Do you know if the same weapon was used to kill both our victims?' Nick enquired.

'I'm afraid not. Ballistic forensics should be able to help you with that. But I did retrieve this.' Amis went over to a steel dish, took some metallic tweezers and held up a lump of metal. To Ruth's untrained eye, it looked the same as the bullet Amis had retrieved from Aaron's body.

'At a guess,' Ruth said, '… it's the same ammunition.'

'Correct. Ten points, starter for ten, no conferring,' he joked, mimicking a BBC quiz show. 'This bullet is a 9mm, and so were all the bullets that I managed to retrieve from your male victim.'

'Okay,' Nick said with a shrug. 'I feel like you want to show us something, Tony?'

'I do indeed.' He pointed at the bodies. 'What do you see when you look at your two victims?'

Ruth had no idea what Amis was getting at.

'Two victims of gunshot wounds?' Ruth asked with some hesitation.

'Yes,' Amis agreed, 'but there is a major difference.'

Ruth looked at the bodies again and then something struck her about the wounds. 'Natalie was killed with a gunshot to the head at close range, execution style.' She then pointed to Aaron's body. 'Aaron was shot five times. In the leg, the stomach and the chest.'

'Exactly,' he said triumphantly. 'Listen, I'm not a firearms or ballistics expert but what does this show?'

Nick shrugged. 'They were shot by different people?'

'Almost certainly. Natalie was murdered by a cold-blooded killer who was used to handling firearms.' He went over to Aaron's body and circulated his hand. 'My guess is that Aaron was killed by someone who had no, or very little, experience of handling weapons. The wounds are scattered.' Amis's gaze flicked from Nick to Ruth. 'In my humble opinion, there is no way Aaron Jenkins was killed by the same person as his wife.'

Ruth gave Nick a dark look. Up until now, they had been working on the assumption that there had only been one killer.

Chapter 39

It had been ten minutes since French and Kennedy had arrived at the PTC Security compound and spotted a Range Rover that they believed belonged to an OCG in Birkenhead. Given that Connor Bradley and Shaun Peterson could well be armed, French had immediately called for backup and explained that they needed AFOs on the scene.

Kennedy gave a frustrated sigh, grabbed the radio, and pressed the grey speak button. 'Control from eight zero, are you receiving, over?'

'Eight zero from Control, we are receiving, go ahead, over,' said the CAD operator.

'Do we have an ETA for ARV and backup at our current location, over,' she asked.

ARV stood for Armed Response Vehicles.

French gave her a look as if to say that they needed armed support right now. But he also knew that they were in the middle of nowhere. Nearly all the ARVs were based in major towns in North Wales so it was going to take some time for them to arrive.

'Eight zero, we do have an ARV en route from Anglesey but I'm getting an ETA of over 30 minutes on that I'm afraid, over.'

'Bollocks,' Kennedy hissed as she glanced over at French. Then she pressed the button on the radio again. 'Control, this is eight zero, received and understood, out.'

She shrugged as she stared at the buildings which housed PTC Security. 'We can't just go over there and try to arrest Gary Williams and present him with a search warrant, can we?'

'Not really,' French said dryly as he buzzed down the window. It was getting hot and stuffy in the car.

Suddenly, the unmistakable sound of a man crying out in pain.

'Help me!' shouted a voice that came from inside one of the buildings.

'Fuck,' Kennedy snapped as she glanced at French. 'What do we do now?'

Opening his door, French gave her a serious look. 'We have to go and have a look. I've got vests in the boot.'

Kennedy looked rattled as she grabbed the radio. 'Control from eight zero, are you receiving, over?'

'Eight zero from Control, we are receiving, go ahead, over.'

'We have reason to believe that a violent crime is in progress. Myself and DS French are going to investigate but will proceed with caution, over.'

'Three eight, received. Please keep your radio channels open, over.'

'Will do, out,' Kennedy replied.

Getting out slowly, French gazed over at the buildings. A few of the windows on the ground floor were open, which wasn't surprising given the weather.

He went to the boot of the Astra and opened it.

Reaching inside, he pulled out DC Garrow's black Kevlar bulletproof jacket and handed it to Kennedy.

'Thanks,' she said, taking it.

Grabbing his own Kevlar jacket, French put it on quickly and fastened the zips and straps so that it was on tight.

'I'd forgotten how heavy these bloody things are,' Kennedy groaned under the weight.

'Yeah, it belongs to DC Jim Garrow and he's a big bugger,' French joked quietly. He noticed that Kennedy looked anxious. 'You okay?'

She nodded but he wasn't convinced. 'Yeah, come on,' she said, gesturing to the buildings.

They moved forward very slowly.

Since the shout, there had been no sound and no movement from inside.

The trees to the right shook gently in the wind and then stopped as if they had registered their presence.

French heard the faint sound of a tractor in the distance.

The stillness of the compound was making him feel incredibly uneasy.

This is starting to freak me out, he thought to himself.

Then another gentle whoosh as the wind picked up again, and fallen leaves skittered noisily across the ground.

As they continued, the grit and stones crunched under their boots. It sounded incredibly loud in the silence.

There was a glint of light as one of the windows was opened fully.

Someone was watching them from inside.

Shit!

French gestured to Kennedy and then nodded over at the window.

She nodded back to confirm she'd spotted it.

French felt his pulse quicken as they approached the front of the building and the customer entrance.

It's way too quiet, he thought.

Moving slowly over to a ground floor window, he cupped his hands and looked inside.

There was just an empty store room with shelves, a mop and bucket, a hoover, and an aluminium stepladder.

He glanced over to Kennedy who was peering through another window. Then she looked back at him and shook her head to signal that she hadn't seen anything.

French jabbed his finger towards the entrance. They needed to go inside.

Walking gently up the wooden steps, French took hold of the metallic handle, pulled it down, and pushed the door open gingerly.

They went inside and then stopped.

The reception area and desks were deserted.

French listened.

Silence.

Then he heard a metallic clanking sound from further along the building.

There was an interconnecting door to their right, which was the direction that the noise was coming from.

As they moved towards the door, French spotted something on the carpet in front of the interconnecting door.

Spots of fresh blood.

Kennedy saw them too.

As French warily opened the door, the handle squeaked.

Bloody hell!

They both froze and held their breath.

He pushed the door open and saw feet, then legs, on the laminate flooring in front of them.

There was a body on the ground.

French recognised the Timberland boots from before.

It was Gary Williams.

As they approached, they saw that Gary was lying on his back staring up at the ceiling.

There was a dark, reddy-black hole the size of a fifty pence piece between his eyes. On the floor around his head was a splattering of brains and blood.

Jesus!

He had been murdered in an almost identical fashion to Natalie Jenkins.

French exchanged a dark look with Kennedy. There was no way they could radio in what they'd found and risk being heard.

The noise was getting louder. It sounded like someone was moving metal – almost like the sound of someone stacking chairs.

What the hell is that?

With another signal, they moved across the room to another interconnecting door. It sounded as if whatever was going on, it was going on behind the door.

French reached out his hand to the aluminium door handle. Then he took a deep breath to steady himself. His palms were sweaty.

He shot a look over at Kennedy to check she was ready. She gave him a nod.

Pushing down the handle quietly, French opened the door inch by inch so as not to alert anyone to their presence. He took a nervous swallow.

The door led into what looked to be an enormous store room that went up into the roof. It was lit only by a skylight and was dark and shadowy.

On the far side of the room, two figures were loading items into a series of black kit bags.

The two figures were wearing balaclavas.

Peering intently into the darkness, French saw they were loading automatic weapons and steel boxes of ammunition.

He took a step forward and Kennedy came to his side.

Fishing out his warrant card, French stood up straight and held it up. He wasn't sure if this was suicidal, but this was part of the job. His heart was thumping hard against his chest like a drum.

'North Wales Police! Stay where you are!' he yelled at the top of his voice.

The two men looked startled for a second.

'Stop there and move back!' Kennedy thundered as they both took a few steps towards the men.

'Fuck off!' the larger man said in a thick Scouse accent. 'Bizzy scum.'

He then pulled a Glock 17 handgun from his waistband, aimed it in their direction, and fired.

CRACK!

French instinctively dived out of the way.

As he crashed to the ground, he saw that Kennedy had crumpled to the floor and was now lying on her back.

Shit!

Jumping up, he scurried over to where she was lying. She wasn't moving.

Oh no no …

He looked down at her, searching her face. Her eyes opened and she sucked in a breath.

Then she winced in pain as she put her hand to the bulletproof vest.

There was a bullet hole at the centre of her chest.

Thank God!

'I'm all right,' she gasped, 'just winded.'

The vest had saved her life.

'Christ.' French shook his head and then glanced back.

The two men were now making their way to the door outside with the heavy kit bags.

'Hang on … and take deep breaths,' French told her as he unclipped the straps around her vest. 'Better?' he asked, now that the vest was a little looser.

'Yeah.' Kennedy nodded but she was clearly shaken.

French clicked his radio but Kennedy put her hand up. 'Don't you dare call for a paramedic. I'm just winded. I'll get the FME to look at me when we get back.'

Now that French was sure that Kennedy was okay, he needed to check on what was going on outside and let Control know. After all, there was an ARV on its way, and the suspect had fired at police officers without a moment's hesitation.

'I'll be back in a minute,' he reassured her as he got up and jogged over to the exit where the men had left.

'Where the hell are you going?' Kennedy gasped, sounding concerned.

'I'm just having a look. I'll be fine.'

As French came out into the daylight, he squinted for a second and tried to adjust his eyes.

Over to his left, the two men were jumping into the black Range Rover and slamming the doors.

French clicked his radio. 'Control from eight zero, are you receiving, over?'

The Range Rover reversed at high speed out from where it had parked in the shade, its engine whining loudly.

'Control to eight zero, receiving, go ahead, over.'

'Shot fired at officers, no casualties. Suspects are leaving current location in a black Range Rover, registration Delta Alpha one nine, Whiskey Tango Charlie. Be advised, suspects are armed and dangerous, over.'

Suddenly, the Range Rover turned and sped back

across the car park towards where French was standing. The tyres threw up a huge cloud of dirt and dust as they went.

Oh shit! French's stomach lurched. He had fully expected the men to drive away.

Taking a few steps back, he braced himself to dive in case they tried to shoot him from the car.

Instead, the Range Rover skidded to an abrupt stop in the dirt.

French froze in fear.

What the hell are they doing?

He held his breath.

The passenger door opened and one of the balaclavered men marched the ten yards towards him, pointing a Glock 17 at his head.

'You're scared now, aren't you bizzy, eh?' he taunted him with a sneer.

French could feel his pulse pounding and his mouth was dry. Was the man just going to shoot him there in cold blood?

The man got to about three yards away. Even though he was wearing a black balaclava, French could see that he was smirking. His eyes were dark brown.

'I tell you what, you've got some balls coming out here after us armed only with your tiny cock,' the man mocked.

Then he pointed the gun about ten feet above French's head and fired.

CRACK!

French flinched. He felt sick with fear.

'Tell you what bizzy,' the man snarled. 'Next time I see you, I'm gonna blow your fucking brains out. And that is a promise.'

The man turned, calmly marched back towards the

Range Rover, got in, and they sped away out of the compound.

Kennedy came out of the door behind French. She had taken off her vest but looked a little unsteady on her feet.

'Oh my God, are you okay?' she asked as she approached. Her eyes were wide with fear.

French nodded, but he was shaking all over.

'I heard a gunshot,' she said as she put a hand on his arm.

French blew out his cheeks. 'It's okay. I'm okay.'

Chapter 40

Ruth was studying the scene board which was now cluttered with photographs, maps, writing and other documents. She had sent both French and Kennedy down to the FME – forensic medical examiner – to be checked over. Even though they had insisted they were both okay when they arrived back in Llancastell, Ruth wasn't taking any chances. They had been shot at which would have been terrifying.

Sipping at her bottle of water, she knew that she now had three murders on her hands and it felt like the case was escalating at breakneck speed. She'd already had a call from the Chief Constable of North Wales Police as the national media were now following events. She reassured him that they had a strong line of enquiry as well as suspects. The names and photos of Connor Bradley and Shaun Peterson had now been released to the press and media with the information that they were wanted by police in connection with all three murders. There was also a warning that they were armed and incredibly dangerous and should not be approached.

Ruth turned and looked back into the CID office which was a hive of activity. She caught Georgie's eye. 'Have we had any luck with that Range Rover?'

Georgie shook her head. 'No, boss. All units have got the details. We've also put the registration onto the ANPR system but no one seems to have seen it anywhere.'

'Okay, thank you,' Ruth said, now deep in thought. 'Keep me posted.'

'Yes, boss,' Georgie replied.

Ruth looked around at her team. 'Right guys. We need every available ARV in the area on standby. Connor Bradley and Shaun Peterson need to be stopped before they kill anyone else. Any news on getting the chopper up to help us?'

She was referring to the one police helicopter that North Wales Police shared with Cheshire. The EC145 was controlled by the National Police Air Service – NPAS.

Garrow looked over and shook his head. 'There's a major incident involving a car chase close to Rhyl. Once they've dealt with that, they'll let us know.'

Ruth gave a frustrated sigh. The cuts to police budgets was starting to have a real impact on their ability to do their job effectively. There were two armed and very dangerous men somewhere in North Wales wanted for three brutal murders. They had the make of car and the registration but they couldn't use air support as they only had one shared helicopter.

Looking at her watch, Ruth realised that she was going to need to do a press conference. She'd had a call from the North Wales Police media unit at St Asaph. They were being swamped with demands for information and updates on the murders.

'Georgie?' Ruth said as she went over to her. 'Can you liaise with the media officer at St Asaph?' She glanced at her watch. 'I'll do a press conference at 7pm so that there's time for it to hit the 9pm national and local news.'

'Yes, boss,' Georgie replied as she reached over and grabbed the phone.

Ruth's head was spinning as she wandered back into her office, sat down, and tried to piece together everything that had happened in the past few days.

Her computer beeped to signal that an email had been received. She clicked her mouse to see if it was important enough to warrant reading immediately. She had requested the military records of Aaron Jenkins.

Opening the files that had arrived, she saw something that caught her eye. In 2013, Aaron Jenkins, Ian Bellamy and Gary Williams had all been investigated by the DSCU – the Defence Serious Crime Unit. It was a unit that dealt with any criminal activity within the British Armed Forces. There had been an allegation from an organisation called *Human Rights Watch*, a charity set up to expose the abuse of human rights around the world. It was alleged that in August 2007, all three had been involved in an unlawful killing of a civilian at a town called Bakhsh Abad in Helmand Province in Afghanistan. There was pressure on the British Army to investigate all three men for this war crime and for them to be brought to trial. According to the records, the allegation was never proved and there wasn't enough evidence for them to ever stand trial for the killing.

Although Ruth couldn't see how this event had anything to do with the three murders that she was investigating, it seemed curious that they were all linked by this event.

Her phone rang. Glancing down, she saw that it was the hospital.

'Hello, DI Hunter?' she said, answering the call.

'Hi, this is Dr Hillman at the ICU. I wanted to let you

know that Ian Bellamy regained consciousness about ten minutes ago.'

'How is he?' she asked.

'Groggy and confused,' Dr Hillman replied.

'I could do with one of my officers questioning him this evening, if that's possible,' Ruth said. 'It's important.'

Bellamy was at the centre of this firearms trafficking and they needed as much intel on Connor Bradley and Shaun Peterson as they could get.

'He's very tired but I've seen the news so I know what's happening,' Dr Hillman replied. 'I agree that it is important that you talk to him.'

'Thank you,' Ruth said gratefully. 'Just to check, my armed officer is still outside his room, isn't he?'

'Oh yes,' Dr Hillman responded. 'He hasn't moved.'

'Good. I'll send someone over right now. Thank you for calling.'

'No problem.'

She ended the call.

Out of the corner of her eye, Ruth spotted French and Kennedy coming back into the CID office. They headed over to her door.

'You two okay?' she asked, getting up from her seat with a concerned expression.

Kennedy nodded to French. 'Dan saved my life. I'm not sure I would have thought of putting on a vest before going into that building.'

Ruth pulled a fretful face. 'What did the FME say?'

'Nothing more serious than a bruised rib,' Kennedy explained with a shrug.

'You should both be at home after an incident like that. It must have shaken you up?'

French shook his head with a serious expression.

'Speaking for myself, boss, I'm not going anywhere until we've got those two psychopaths locked up.'

Kennedy smiled at him. 'I couldn't have put it better.'

For a moment, Ruth thought she detected a little frisson of attraction between the two of them. *Interesting*, she thought to herself. She always felt that French deserved to be in a relationship with someone nice. He was a decent man − and there weren't many of those around in her experience.

'In that case, can you two do me a favour? Ian Bellamy has regained consciousness. Can you guys go over to the hospital and question him?'

French and Kennedy looked at each other and nodded in unison.

'We're on it, boss,' French assured her as they turned and left.

Chapter 41

Ruth looked at her watch. It was 7pm. She looked out at the press conference with some trepidation. In the space of 48 hours, this had gone from a local story about a farmer being shot, to a triple murder with rumours of gangs, automatic weapons, and firearms trafficking to the major OCGs of Liverpool. It was now running as a story on all the major television and news channels. The room was packed with half a dozen camera crews set up over to her left.

On the table in front of her was a jug of water and several small digital recorders and microphones that eager journalists had placed there. A woman in her late 30s, Asian, smartly dressed, made her way over to where Ruth was sitting and gave her a friendly smile.

'DI Hunter?' she asked quietly.

Ruth gave her a quizzical look. She had no idea who she was. 'Yes?'

'I'm Samira Chandra,' she explained politely. 'I'm the new Chief Corporate Communications Officer for North

Wales Police. I've just come from the main press office at St Asaph.'

Ruth frowned. 'Oh right. I was expecting Kerry Mahoney,' she said, although the news that there was a new Chief Communications Officer was music to her ears. Kerry had always been a rather unpleasant, spiky woman in Ruth's limited experience.

Samira pulled a face. 'I guess that you didn't hear. Kerry had a stroke a few months ago. She's very unwell.'

Ruth instantly felt guilty at her previous thoughts. 'I'm sorry to hear that,' she said. If she was honest, she wasn't sorry that she no longer had to deal with Kerry.

Samira sat down, pulled in her chair, and turned to Ruth. 'This has all escalated very quickly, hasn't it?'

'Yes, unfortunately.'

'Anything you need from me at this stage?' Samira asked in a genuinely helpful tone – it was a refreshing change.

'I don't think so. Just if the questions get out of hand, if you can step in?'

'Of course, no problem.'

'Right, here we go then,' Ruth whispered as she turned to the room. 'Good evening everyone. I'm Detective Inspector Ruth Hunter and I am the senior investigating officer on this investigation. Next to me is Samira Chandra, our Chief Corporate Communications Officer for North Wales. I want to update you on developments in the last seventy-two hours as this is a fast-moving case. I can confirm that we're currently investigating three extremely violent murders that have taken place in the past few days. The first of these took place on Monday afternoon at Manor Farm, just outside Llangollen, when Aaron Jenkins was shot and killed. His wife Natalie was abducted and also shot dead yesterday. And this morning a third victim, Gary Williams, was shot and killed at a location just outside Corwen. These were horrific, cold-blooded crimes against three defenceless people. We are appealing for witnesses for all of these attacks, and we'd like to speak to any members of the public who were in those areas at those specific times or saw anything suspicious.' Ruth cleared her throat and continued. 'We are currently working closely with the Merseyside Police Organised Crime Task Force. As a result, we have two suspects who we would like to talk to in connection with all three murders.' Ruth looked over as two photographs appeared on the large screens that flanked the stage of the press conference room. 'Connor Bradley and Shaun Peterson. We believe that it is very likely that these two men are responsible for at least two of these murders, so we are appealing for members of the public who might know their whereabouts to ring our hotline. However, these men are armed and incredibly dangerous, so please do not attempt to approach them under any circumstances. I can reassure you that North Wales Police is absolutely committed to finding them, and we are using every resource available to us to bring this investigation to a conclusion as quickly as possible. I do have a couple of minutes if there are any questions.'

Ruth braced herself. This was the most challenging part of any press conference as it required her to think on her feet.

A young female journalist at the front of the room indicated that she wanted to ask a question and Samira nodded in her direction.

'Diane Morante, *Daily Express*,' she said. 'With three very violent attacks in the Llangollen area, can you reassure the town and holidaymakers that they are safe? Or are you advising people to stay away from the area where the attacks took place?'

'My advice would be for the residents of Llangollen to be as vigilant as they normally would be,' Ruth said, trying to remain as vague as she could, 'but we are not advising anyone to stay away from the area.'

Samira held her hand up and announced in a commanding voice, 'I'm afraid that's all we have time for at the moment. Thank you.'

Ruth looked at her and said quietly, 'I would have been happy to answer a couple more questions.'

Samira gave her a knowing look. 'I'm sure that you have far more pressing things to do than answer questions that will probably be designed to hint that you're not doing enough to apprehend these men.'

Ruth gave her a surprised look. 'You know what? I do have better things to do. Thank you, Samira.'

Samira shrugged. 'That's what I'm here for.'

Well, she's a breath of fresh air, Ruth thought.

Chapter 42

The sun was beginning to set as French and Kennedy parked their car at the hospital. Visiting hours were over and there was a steady stream of people and cars leaving the site.

Getting out of the car, French looked up at the old hospital buildings. There had been a hospital on this site for over a hundred years.

'I was born here,' he said as they made their way across the car park towards the main entrance. Then he pointed over to the right on the first floor. 'Maternity unit used to be up there. Over nine pounds apparently.'

Kennedy laughed as they went inside. 'Woah, your poor mum!'

'She said she was full of drugs. My dad was watching a Wrexham football game over in Yorkshire somewhere. In fact I don't think he rocked up until the day after.' French felt a twinge of sadness as he said it. His father hadn't shown much interest in him throughout his life, even when he was born.

'My mum was a midwife until she passed,' Kennedy

commented as they reached the lifts on the ground floor, 'at St Thomas' Hospital. They all called it Tommy's. Across the Thames from Big Ben and the Houses of Parliament. I used to love looking out of the windows when I visited her there.'

'Were you and your mum close?' French asked.

'Yeah, very,' she replied with a thoughtful look as they got into the lift. 'What about your parents?'

'How do you mean?'

'Are you guys close?'

He shook his head. 'No, not really. I see them once in a blue moon to be honest. It's just the way things are I suppose.'

'That's sad.'

French gave a shrug. 'I'm used to it now.'

She raised an eyebrow inquisitively. 'It doesn't get to you?'

'No,' he replied, but then he actually thought about it. And for some reason he felt at ease talking honestly with Kennedy. It felt comfortable – even safe. 'That's a lie actually,' he admitted with a self-effacing smile. 'I try to pop in at Christmas, but I know they're not bothered if I do or don't. Sometimes I get a birthday card and sometimes I don't. And when I see or hear about other people with their parents and family, it hurts a bit. But there's nothing I can do. That was the hand I was dealt.' French stopped talking because he was starting to feel the emotion of it well inside him.

Kennedy gave him an empathetic look. 'I'm sorry to hear that.'

The doors clanked open. They came out of the lift into a wide corridor and turned right towards the ICU. French was now concerned that he'd revealed too much, or that he'd made a fool of himself by being so honest.

SIMON MCCLEAVE

'Sorry, I didn't mean to drone on like that,' he said as they walked.

'Don't apologise.' Kennedy gave him a reassuring smile. 'I admire a man who can be honest about how he feels.'

Their eyes met, and they both smiled.

French felt his pulse quicken for a second. *She's lovely.*

Turning into the ICU, they took out their warrant cards in case they needed them.

French pressed the buzzer and then held his warrant card up to the camera so that the nurses could see it.

The white door clunked, and they went inside.

A doctor in his early 40s, with a mop of sandy hair and wearing glasses, approached. 'I'm Dr Hillman. I spoke to DI Hunter earlier,' he said.

'DC Kennedy and DS French,' French said as they showed their warrant cards.

'As I explained,' Dr Hillman said in a serious tone, 'Ian is very tired and disoriented. I'd appreciate it if you could keep your time with him to a minimum, please.'

Kennedy nodded. 'No problem.'

'Thank you.'

'Is he on his own?' French asked.

'No, his ex-wife Sheila is in there with him.'

'Okay.' They walked towards the corridor where Ian Bellamy's room was located.

French immediately spotted O'Hara, the authorised firearms officer, sitting on a chair outside his room.

'DC Kennedy and DS French, Llancastell CID,' Kennedy said as they flashed their warrant cards again.

'Everything been okay?' French asked quietly.

'Not a peep,' the AFO replied. 'He's got a visitor at the moment. His ex-wife, but that's the only one he's had. I checked her ID before she went in.'

'Good. Thank you,' French said as they went to the door, opened it, and peered inside.

Bellamy was lying in the bed hooked up to an ECG and a drip. His face was swollen and bruised from the accident.

A woman in her late 40s, red hair, too much makeup, was sitting on a chair by the side of the bed.

'Ian Bellamy?' French said as he and Kennedy stepped into the room and closed the door behind them. 'We're detectives from Llancastell CID.'

'Right,' Bellamy said, looking confused.

'We'd like to ask you a couple of questions if that's okay?'

'He's still a bit out of it, aren't you love?' Sheila said from where she was sitting. Then she got up. 'I'll go and get a brew and leave you to it, eh?'

Kennedy gave her a half-smile. 'Thank you,' she said gently.

French and Kennedy went and sat down on two grey plastic chairs beside the bed.

'Do you remember the accident, Ian?' he asked.

Bellamy shook his head slowly. 'No.' His voice was croaky.

Kennedy gestured to the plastic jug of water. 'Would you like some water?'

Bellamy nodded, but then winced in pain.

'We were the officers who were pursuing you,' French explained, 'and then we pulled you out.'

Bellamy took the plastic cup of water that Kennedy had poured for him and took a sip.

'You saved my life then?' he said in a sardonic tone.

'I'm not sure about that, but we do need to ask you a few questions.'

Bellamy shrugged with a dry expression. 'I'm not going anywhere, am I?'

'We went to your house. And we found all the guns, the parts, 3D printer, the plans. We know what you were doing and who you were doing it with.'

Bellamy's face visibly fell. He didn't say anything and looked away.

Kennedy, who had taken out her notebook and pen, said quietly, 'We're going to need you to tell us about the men you were selling firearms to.'

Bellamy smirked. 'I have no idea what you're talking about. I was making those guns for myself. I'm ex-military and I collect guns.'

French gave an audible sigh even though he wasn't surprised that Bellamy wasn't going to cooperate. 'Come on, Ian. You were manufacturing the same gun over and over again. A Skorpion submachine gun.'

Bellamy narrowed his eyes. 'I don't know what to tell you. I like that gun.'

Kennedy looked at French and rolled her eyes.

'We know you were supplying Connor Bradley and Shaun Peterson,' French said.

'Never heard of them,' Bellamy said unconvincingly, but he was clearly rattled.

'Really? You really want to play it like this, Ian?'

'I don't know what you want me to say,' he sneered. 'I don't know who or what you're talking about.'

French waited for a few seconds. Bellamy had left him no choice but to reveal all that had happened while he'd been in a coma.

'Ian, I've got some very bad news for you, I'm afraid,' he said quietly. 'Your friend, Gary Williams, was shot and killed earlier today.'

'What?' Bellamy was visibly upset.

'Myself and DC Kennedy were there when it happened, and we know that the two men who murdered Gary were Connor Bradley and Shaun Peterson. They also murdered Aaron and his wife Natalie.'

There was silence as Bellamy tried to take it all in.

Suddenly, an alarm started to sound from somewhere in the hospital. It sounded like a fire alarm.

French and Kennedy looked at each other and then got up.

French went over to the door and opened it. The noise was much louder out in the corridor.

O'Hara was now standing.

'It's the fire alarm,' he shouted over the din to French.

'Is it a drill?'

'Not that I know of,' he replied, and then gestured down the corridor. 'Let me go and find out what's going on.'

French went back into the room. The noise of the alarm was going to prevent them questioning Bellamy in any meaningful way.

'I can't believe that Gary is dead,' Bellamy said under his breath as if talking to himself.

Kennedy wandered over to the door and looked out of the small glass panel. Then she glanced back at French. 'There's a lot of activity out there.'

She opened the door and O'Hara poked his head inside and spoke to French. 'There's a fire in one of the storage rooms out in the corridor. It's filling everywhere with smoke. Okay if I go and see if I can help?'

'Yeah, go on.'

'I'll go and see what's going on,' Kennedy told French.

They left, and French sat down on the chair next to the bed. 'Looks like it's just me and you now.'

Bellamy was still lost in thought.

The alarm was starting to grate and give French a headache. He sighed, got up and went over to the door again to see what was happening. Through the glass panel he could see that the corridor outside was now deserted.

Suddenly, a figure appeared.

Before French could react, the door was opened forcefully and smashed into him. Losing his footing, he tumbled to the floor.

A figure came into the room and kicked him in the head. French saw stars for a moment.

Jesus Christ!

Trying to get back on his feet, French saw the figure over by the bed.

A man in a black balaclava.

It was the man who had threatened him earlier that day.

CRACK!

The deafening sound of a gunshot.

French scrambled to his feet only to see that the man had shot Ian Bellamy in the face and he was now probably dead.

Jesus!

The man turned and squared up to French.

Raising the Glock 17 so that it was level with French's head, the man growled, 'I promised you the next time I saw you I was gonna blow your fucking brains out. And a promise is promise.'

French felt his stomach lurch in terror.

He could see the man's eyes staring out through the black material of the balaclava. He looked like he was almost smirking.

French wasn't about to stand there and get shot in the head.

Fuck this!

Pushing his feet against the floor, he launched himself at the man, hitting his arm just as the Glock fired. The bullet whistled past French's head and into the wall.

The Glock flew out of the man's hand onto the floor and skidded under the bed.

French and the man began grappling with each other and fell to the floor.

The man rolled on top of French and then punched him hard on the jaw. French was dazed but knew that the man was going to kill him unless he could overpower him.

Using his legs, French used everything he had to throw the man off of him. At the same time, he grabbed at the man's balaclava and it came off.

A face he recognised looked up at him from the floor.

Connor Bradley.

French tried to pin Bradley down on the floor but he was too strong.

Bradley reached out and grabbed French's throat with an iron-like grip.

French tried to release Bradley's hand but he couldn't breathe. He was starting to feel dizzy.

He had no choice but to punch Bradley with his right hand. He connected with his temple and knocked him flying.

Getting to his feet, French glanced at the door. He needed Kennedy or the AFO to come in right now and help.

Bradley got up and stared at French who was now between him and the door.

'Out my way, bizzy,' he snarled.

French shook his head. 'No chance.'

Bradley ran at French and shoulder-barged him into the door. The metallic handle went into the base of French's spine and winded him.

Staggering to one side and gasping for breath, he watched helplessly as Bradley opened the door and sprinted out.

French gritted his teeth. There was no way he was going to let him get away.

He followed him, and saw Bradley running away down the corridor to his left.

He chased after him.

The fire alarm had now stopped screeching.

With his feet clattering noisily on the floor, French saw Bradley disappear around a corner.

French came hurtling around the corner but the corridor ahead was somehow deserted.

Where the hell did he go?

Gasping for breath, he spotted a door with a green 'fire exit' sign above it.

He grabbed the handle and pulled the door open.

Below, there was the sound of footsteps running down the stairs.

French continued his pursuit, leaping down the steps as fast as he could, hoping he didn't lose his balance.

As he reached the final set of steps, he saw that Bradley was pushing and pulling at the double fire exit doors but they were locked.

'Stay there!' French gasped, trying to get his breath.

Bradley spun around and fixed French with an aggressive stare. 'Oh do fuck off, bizzy. You're starting to really get on my nerves.'

French stared back at him as he came slowly down the steps towards him. 'You're not going anywhere.'

The expression on Bradley's face changed.

'Wanna bet?' he said with a cold sneer. He reached around his back and pulled a seven-inch serrated hunting knife from the waistband of his trousers.

Oh shit.

Before French could move back up the steps, Bradley had marched towards him and plunged the knife into his abdomen.

Jesus.

Bradley pulled the knife out and stabbed him again. Then he looked French in the face. 'I told you I'd have you, bizzy.'

Bradley jogged away up the stairs.

French crumpled and fell down the final two steps onto the concrete floor. Trying to sit up, he put his hand to his stomach. His blood was warm and wet on his skin.

His head started to spin as he tried to get his breath.

Then everything went black.

Chapter 43

Ruth and Nick raced across Llancastell with the blues and twos going as they weaved in and out of the evening traffic at high speed. It had been ten minutes since Kennedy had called to tell them that Ian Bellamy had been shot and killed while she and the AFO had been distracted by a fire. However, she had left French with Bellamy and there had been no sign of French since. Ruth could feel the anxiety in her gut of having an officer missing, with a gunman loose in the hospital.

She hit the redial button on her phone as she tried to call French yet again. It rang out.

'Nothing?' Nick asked with a dark expression.

Ruth shook her head as she reached for the car's radio. 'Control from three six, are you receiving, over?'

'Control to three six, receiving, go ahead.'

'Our ETA to Llancastell Hospital is five minutes. I need a status update on units in attendance, over,' Ruth said as they swerved and then sped down the outside of the traffic waiting at a red light.

'Control to three six. We have two uniformed patrols on site, one ARV with an ETA of ten minutes and a second one within twenty minutes, over.'

'Okay, thank you.' Ruth could feel the adrenaline coursing through her veins. 'Can we reiterate that the suspects are armed and incredibly dangerous? We are looking for a black Range Rover Sport, registration Delta Alpha one nine, Whiskey Tango Charlie, over.'

'Control to three six, received and understood, over.'

Nick glanced at her with an urgent look. 'The hospital CCTV,' he said.

She knew exactly what he meant as she reached for her phone and called Kennedy.

'Jade?'

'Boss?'

'Any sign of Dan yet?' Ruth asked anxiously.

'No, boss.' She sounded upset. 'Uniformed officers are searching the hospital.'

'You okay?'

'I shouldn't have left him.' Kennedy sounded distraught.

'He'll be fine,' Ruth reassured her. They could go into the details of where she went wrong when the dust settled. 'Is the pathologist there yet?'

'Just arrived. I've got this part of the ICU sealed off with uniformed officers. Only essential medical staff are in and out.'

'I need you to get down to the security office on the ground floor as quickly as possible. Check their CCTV. See if you can see the gunman and Dan.'

'I'm on it now, boss,' Kennedy said, and ended the call.

Nick screeched at high speed around the roundabout as they turned towards the hospital. It was now only about two minutes away but Ruth felt sick with anxiety. Her head was spinning as she tried to juggle all that had happened and how to respond to it.

She grabbed the radio again. 'Control from three six, are you receiving, over?'

'Control to three six, receiving, go ahead, over.'

'I'm going to need every available officer over here as soon as possible. I want a cordon set up on all roads around the hospital and the car park. And I want a road block on the A483. Every vehicle needs to be checked, over.'

'Three six, received and understood, over.'

They came hurtling into the hospital car park. There were now three marked police patrol cars parked at the front of the entrance with their blue lights flashing, along with an ambulance on stand by.

They screeched to a halt and jumped out, then ran towards the main doors into the hospital. The building was now effectively in lockdown as the gunman could still be somewhere inside. The safety of patients and staff was of paramount importance. There were several uniformed officers in the foyer explaining to staff that there was going to be strict monitoring of all members of the public entering and exiting the building.

Nick gestured to the main security office where the CCTV monitors were housed. 'This way, isn't it?'

Ruth nodded as they jogged across the foyer, flashing their warrant cards as they went so they didn't have to explain to anyone who they were.

As they reached the security office, Ruth saw that the door was wide open.

Kennedy was sitting with two security guards as they peered intently at the bank of CCTV monitors on the wall.

'What have we got?' Ruth asked impatiently, even though she knew that Kennedy could have only been in there a matter of minutes. But time was critical. If French was injured or in trouble, every second was invaluable.

'There!' Kennedy said loudly as she pointed to a screen.

Ruth rushed over and saw an image of French pursuing a man along a corridor.

'Is that the only sighting we've got of Dan?' Nick asked.

Kennedy nodded. 'So far.'

'Where is that?' Ruth asked one of the guards.

'It's at the far end of the ICU. I'll show you.'

'Okay, come on,' Ruth said, and then turned to Kennedy. 'Keep looking. I need to know where Dan is and we need to know if that suspect is still in this building.'

'Yes, boss.'

Ruth, Nick and the guard ran across the foyer and towards the door to the staircase.

Crashing through the door, they bounded up the stairs.

Ruth was taking the steps two at a time, even though the muscles in her legs started to ache.

First floor.

They turned again.

Grabbing the rail to keep her balance, Ruth was now sucking for air.

She didn't care. French was missing and needed to be found.

Come on Ruth, keep going!

Looking up, she saw the door to the second floor.

They yanked the door open and came out into a corridor. There was a strong smell of acrid smoke where there had been a fire. Ruth assumed it had been started deliberately to distract officers from protecting Ian Bellamy.

There were a couple of fire officers and uniformed officers milling about.

'This way,' the guard panted as they continued to run.

Jesus. Ruth's lungs were now burning.

They sprinted through the main doors into the ICU which were open and being manned by more police officers.

Then down a corridor, past the room where Ian Bellamy had been shot, and round a corner.

Ruth recognised this as where the CCTV had picked up French chasing the suspect.

They slowed as they looked around. Had French continued to chase the man down this corridor?

There was a hospital room to their right with an empty bed and furniture. Ruth went inside and scanned around but there was nothing of note in there.

They continued to march down the corridor.

Up on their right was a door marked *Fire Exit* but there was also a smaller sign that read *Not in use – No access to outside.*

Nick went to the door. 'Worth a look?' he suggested.

She nodded, although she couldn't see why they would have gone down a staircase that led nowhere.

Nick looked down on the floor just where the door opened. 'Boss, there's a speck of blood here.' He crouched down and looked closely. 'Yeah, it's fresh.'

Ruth's heart sank. She feared that something was very wrong.

Nick led the way as they hurried down the fire exit stairs.

'Boss!' he shouted, and as Ruth turned a corner she saw a figure lying at the bottom of the staircase.

It was French.

Oh God no!

Nick raced over, crouched down and felt for a pulse. 'It's okay, mate. We're here. We've got you.' He looked up at Ruth. 'I've got a pulse but it's very faint.'

Chapter 44

Ruth and Nick were now standing with Kennedy in the ICU. There was an uncomfortable silence. French was having an emergency operation, but he had lost a great deal of blood. Meanwhile, SOCOs in their white forensic suits were coming and going from Bellamy's room which was now a crime scene. His body had been removed from the room and taken down to the mortuary where there would be a post-mortem. The cause of death was clearly a bullet through the brain but protocol was protocol.

'Oscar five to three six, over,' said a voice on Ruth's radio. Oscar five was the call sign for the inspector who was in charge of the trained firearms unit that was sweeping the hospital. Kennedy had continued to scour the CCTV downstairs and identified the man who French had been chasing as Connor Bradley.

'Oscar five, this is three six, go ahead, over.'

'We have made a thorough sweep of the hospital,' the inspector informed her. 'There are no signs of the suspect anywhere, over.'

'Okay, thank you. Out,' Ruth replied with some sense

of relief – but also some frustration. She was glad there wasn't a dangerous gunman roaming around the hospital. But it was frustrating that Bradley had been able to cause a distraction, shoot Bellamy, stab French, and get away undetected.

Kennedy looked nervously over towards the direction of the operating theatre where French was being treated. 'If anything happens to Dan, I'll never forgive myself. I can't believe I left him.'

'It's okay,' Ruth tried to reassure her. Her anger was directed more towards O'Hara who was the AFO.

'I can't imagine how he's feeling,' Nick said quietly.

O'Hara was sitting down on some nearby chairs staring down at the ground. He had left his post, and the suspect he'd been charged with protecting had been murdered. And a police officer was now fighting for his life in a nearby operating theatre.

Ruth was struggling to find much sympathy for him as she went over.

'Sergeant O'Hara,' she said, looking down at him. 'Why don't you go home now? Just make sure your notes and statement are typed up first thing.'

He shook his head. 'I need to know how DS French is.'

'I'll let you know how the operation goes,' she told him. 'It's okay. You should go now.'

Ruth knew that there would be a thorough investigation, and the IOPC – the Independent Office for Police Conduct – would be called in. O'Hara would be lucky to keep his job given the severity of the repercussions of him leaving Bellamy unprotected. Either that or he'd find himself, as the cliché went, directing traffic in the arse-end of somewhere.

O'Hara nodded, got up and wandered away sheepishly.

Kennedy's phone rang. She answered it and moved away.

Ruth looked at Nick who was wearing a concerned expression. 'Dan had lost a lot of blood,' he said quietly.

'Dan's very tough. And he's young and fit. He's going to be fine.'

Nick didn't look convinced.

Professor Amis approached in his forensic suit. He pulled down his mask and shook his head. His jovial expression had been replaced by one of shock. 'It's like we're in Bogata, Columbia, not Llancastell, North Wales.'

'I know,' Ruth sighed. 'I've never experienced anything quite this bad before. Not even when gang warfare broke out in South London.'

Nick spoke to Amis. 'I'm assuming that the cause of death is the gunshot wound?'

'As you know, we'll have to do a preliminary post-mortem, but yes, there is a significant gunshot wound to the forehead. Very similar to the wound we found on Natalie Jenkins.' Amis gestured back to the room. 'Right, I'd better get on.'

'Sir,' called a voice. It was a young female scene of crime officer. As she approached, she held up a large, clear plastic bag. Inside was a gun that Ruth instantly recognised as a Glock 17. 'We found this under the victim's bed.'

'Right, thank you,' Amis said. 'If you can log it, we can send it to ballistic forensics.'

'Yes, sir,' the SOCO said as she walked away.

Ruth looked at Nick. 'That explains why Bradley didn't shoot Dan.'

'Maybe there was some kind of fight,' he said, thinking out loud. 'That's how the gun ended up there.'

'Sounds plausible,' Ruth agreed.

'I'd better get on,' Amis said, and then gave Ruth a

dark look. 'I hope you catch these lunatics soon before they shoot anyone else.'

'So do I,' Ruth replied, feeling the growing pressure.

Kennedy came back over and gestured to her phone. 'Boss, that was the security guys downstairs. They've spotted a figure leaving the rear entrance of the hospital at 8.47pm. That figure climbs over a wall and gets into a black Range Rover that is parked on a side road. It's too dark to see the registration.'

Ruth sighed in frustration. They didn't need to know the registration. Connor Bradley and Shaun Peterson had assassinated four people in three days and were still on the run.

Chapter 45

An hour later, Ruth was now pumped full of adrenaline as she walked out of her office and across CID. It was all hands on deck in the search for Connor Bradley and Shaun Peterson. It was being described by the media as the biggest manhunt in the area for years. Ruth had spoken to DS Sophie Kent several times to liaise with Merseyside Police Anti-gang unit, as well as phone calls to the NCA and local police stations across The Wirral and Birkenhead.

For a few seconds she peered at the scene board. There was still something that was bothering her about Aaron Jenkins' murder.

'You look deep in thought, boss,' said a voice behind her.

It was Nick.

She pointed to several of the photos. 'I am. There's still something about Aaron's murder that doesn't sit comfortably with me.'

'After what Amis told us?'

'Sort of. Natalie Jenkins, Gary Williams and Ian Bellamy were killed clinically. Bullet to the head, execution style. Very cold. There is no way that the same person who killed them also shot and killed Aaron Jenkins. He was riddled with bullets, almost as if the gun went off by accident.'

'I've thought about that too. We're going on the theory that all these murders were carried out by Bradley and Peterson to eliminate anyone who was involved in their firearms trafficking business.'

Ruth nodded.

'And we know that Connor Bradley killed Ian Bellamy and Gary Williams by shooting them in the head. It stands to reason that it was also Bradley who murdered Natalie Jenkins. Maybe it was Shaun Peterson who killed Aaron? Maybe he's not used to using an automatic weapon. He pulls the trigger and the bullets spray everywhere.'

For a second, Ruth thought Nick had a good point. 'Yeah, but we still have the strange carving on the back of Aaron's hand. Do Bradley and Peterson strike you as the sort of men who would shoot someone and then hang around to carve some symbol into their hand to prove a point?'

'Not really.'

'And if they did, why didn't they do that to Natalie too? They had plenty of time if they wanted to do the same to her.'

Nick processed what she had said. 'You think that Aaron's murder isn't linked to Bradley and Peterson?'

'My instinct says it's not, but it feels like a huge coincidence if it isn't.'

'Unless there was something about Aaron's murder that set off a chain of events that led to the other murders?'

'Maybe.' Ruth could feel herself getting frustrated. She had four murders to deal with and didn't want to get bogged down in the misgivings she had about the first.

'And if Bradley and Peterson weren't responsible for Aaron's death, then we're looking either at his brother Charlie or Bethan Jones. But I'm not convinced on either of them.'

'No, neither am I,' Ruth agreed.

Georgie signalled to Ruth. 'Boss, the helicopter is on its way over. I've given them all the intel so they'll help with the search.'

'That's great news,' Ruth said as she walked back towards her office.

'And just so you know,' Georgie continued, 'those background checks came back on Bethan Jones and Haji Rafiq.'

'Anything crop up?'

'I haven't had time to look through them yet.'

'Let me know when you do, but it's not a priority at the moment.'

Ruth walked away and noticed that the sky outside had darkened to a uniform grey. Charcoal-coloured clouds were heading in from the west. There was a storm brewing. At least that would bring the temperature down.

Nick caught her attention and shook his head. 'Where the hell are they?' he asked rhetorically.

Ruth sighed. 'I wish I bloody knew.' Then her phone rang.

'DI Hunter?' Ruth said.

'It's DS Kent. Anything your end?'

'Not a peep. It's as if they've vanished into thin air,' Ruth admitted in a frustrated tone.

'I'm sending three ARVs over from Liverpool and

basing them on The Wirral in case they try to head back to their home turf,' Kent said.

'My thinking is that they've got to somehow get out of the country given that every copper north of the Watford Gap is now looking for them. And every media outlet is running this as their major headline news story.'

'You've got ferries going out of Holyhead, haven't you?' Kent asked.

'We have, but I've got an ARV and AFOs all over the port. There's no way they're getting on a ferry tonight.'

'There is something that cropped up earlier.'

'Go on,' Ruth prompted her.

'Connor Bradley's father, Michael, used to be a big noise in the Merseyside gangland of the 90s,' she explained. 'He served fifteen years for manslaughter and drug trafficking. He keeps a pretty low profile now, but according to a reliable covert human intelligence force, he owns a helicopter.'

'Any idea where he keeps it?'

'Not at the moment I'm afraid, but it might be that Michael is going to fly his son and Peterson out of the country. Bit of a long shot, I know.'

'We'll take a long shot at the moment as it's all we've got. Thanks, and I'll keep you posted if I hear anything my end.'

'Same here,' Kent said as she ended the call.

As Ruth turned to head back to her office, Georgie called to her. 'Boss, there's a Leonard Nevin down at reception asking for you.'

Ruth frowned. *I wonder what he wants?* she thought.

'Okay, thanks Georgie. Tell the duty sergeant to put him in the main meeting room and we'll be down in five minutes.'

Ruth approached Nick's desk. 'Leonard Nevin is downstairs. He's asked to see me.'

Nick looked puzzled. 'I wonder what he wants?'

'Me too.' Ruth gestured to the busy office. 'I can't really leave here with all this going on. You okay to go downstairs and find out?'

'No problem.' Nick got up and headed for the door.

Chapter 46

A few minutes later, Nick approached the main meeting room on the ground floor of Llancastell nick. As deputy SIO, his head was whirring. He could also feel the anger growing in the pit of his stomach. Connor Bradley had stabbed Dan French who was now lying in a critical state in the ICU. Nick knew that he wouldn't rest until Bradley and Peterson were safely behind bars for a very long time. As a recovering alcoholic, he knew that he had to be careful when it came to harbouring resentments and anger. Having that festering away would unsettle him and throw him off his recovery. At times like this, he would call his AA sponsor to talk about how he was feeling and get it off his chest.

As he reached the door to the meeting room he tried to get his head back to the task in hand. He'd certainly never worked on a case that was this fast moving before. He could feel his adrenaline surging through his veins.

He walked in and saw Leonard Nevin sitting on the far side of the large oval meeting table. The walls of the meeting room had various photos and emblems hanging on them. A black and white photo of the current Chief Constable of North Wales Police, some older photos of North Wales Police officers through the ages, as well as a small plaque with the names of those officers who had lost their lives in the line of duty.

'Hi there,' Nick said politely as he pulled out a chair and sat down.

'Hello,' Leonard said with a half-smile.

Nick gave him a quizzical look. 'I'm afraid DI Hunter is unavailable at the moment. How can I help, Mr Nevin?'

'Leo, please,' he insisted as he pulled out his iPhone. Then he glanced over at Nick and gave him a dark look. 'I've been watching the news. This thing seems to have escalated very quickly.'

'I'm afraid it has,' Nick agreed.

'Well, I expect you're incredibly busy so I'll get straight to the point and explain why I've come in. As you know, on Monday afternoon I took my wife and two grandchildren on the steam engine from Llangollen station. As we pulled out, my grandson Jack turned on his phone. He said he was going to make a video of us all on the journey for Tik Tok. I've no idea what that is.'

Nick nodded to demonstrate that he was listening intently and for him to continue.

'Anyway, it didn't occur to me until this morning that Jack was filming at the very moment of the shooting. I asked him to bring over his phone and we had a look at the video that he took. And very briefly you can see the two men arguing in the field, although I don't think you can see the actual moment of the shooting. Shall I show you?'

Nick nodded enthusiastically. 'Yes, that would be great.' He knew that any video of this kind could be vital in terms of evidence. It might also help shed some light on his and Ruth's concerns that Aaron Jenkins might have been shot by someone other than Connor Bradley or Shaun Peterson.

Getting up from the table, Nick walked around and sat down next to Leonard who was busy looking at his phone.

'Jack has sent me the video, and he showed me how to get it earlier,' Leonard said with a deep frown of frustration. 'Here we go,' he said triumphantly.

Nick peered closely at the screen as the wobbly video of Leonard and Mary sitting on an old-fashioned, red train seat played out.

Then for a second, the video showed the outside fields going past.

Nick could see two figures in the near distance. 'Can we pause it just there?' he asked.

'Erm, yes. How about that?' Leonard hit the pause button and the image froze.

If he was honest, Nick was a little disappointed. Although there were clearly two figures standing close to each other, the image quality was grainy. There wasn't enough detail to make it significant.

'I hope that's of some use?' Leonard asked.

'It is,' Nick reassured him, 'and thank you for coming in with it. If I give you my number, could you send it over to me now?'

'Yes, of course,' he replied, clearly thrilled that he'd been able to help the investigation in some way.

Nick wondered if the boys in digital forensics could clean up the video and get a better look at the two figures in the field. It didn't seem likely.

Chapter 47

Ruth was trying to coordinate the ongoing manhunt for Bradley and Peterson. Despite several reported sightings of their Range Rover, they still didn't have any idea where they were or where they were heading. Georgie had spoken to Range Rover's head office but, given that the car had stolen plates, there was no way of identifying it or tracking the GPS system inside. They were currently relying on police patrols, an ANPR or CCTV camera, or a member of the general public to identify their location. Ruth knew they weren't stupid enough to use bank cards, cash machines, social media or any mobile phone that they had legitimate contracts for. It would be cash and burner phones all the way. They were pros.

Grabbing the phone, she dialled the number for the ICU at the hospital.

'Hello, ICU?'

'Hi there. This is DI Ruth Hunter. I wanted to check on one of my officers. Dan French?'

'Oh yes, can you hold on for a second?'

'Of course.'

There was a horrible silence at the end of the phone.

Ruth held her breath.

'Hi there. I'm afraid Dan is still critical, but we will ring as soon as there is any change.'

'Okay, thank you,' she said quietly as she ended the call.

Even though French was still not out of the woods, there was a terrible moment when Ruth had feared the worst.

There was a knock on her open door which broke her train of thought.

It was Kennedy.

'Any news on Dan?' she asked anxiously.

Ruth shook her head. 'Sorry, no change, but I'll tell you as soon as I hear anything.'

'Thank you, boss,' she replied. Ruth could see that the incident at the hospital and her guilt for leaving French with Bellamy was really taking its toll.

Before Ruth could look back to her desk, Nick came in with a sense of urgency. She knew the look he had when he was on to something.

He sat down and beamed at her. 'I think we've struck gold. We've never managed to find Natalie Jenkins' mobile phone at the farmhouse.'

Ruth shook her head. 'No.'

'And I checked all the forensics from where she was found at Nant Mill. There was no sign of her phone on her body or anywhere nearby.'

'Okay.' Ruth was with him so far.

'So, I got to thinking ...'

'Always a dangerous thing,' she quipped.

'Ha ha,' he groaned, but he was eager to get on. 'What if Natalie deliberately left her phone in Bradley and Peterson's Range Rover? Maybe she thought we'd be able to track it. Or maybe she dropped it in the car when they were bundling her in or dragging her out and they just haven't noticed.'

Ruth raised her eyebrow. 'You think we should track her phone's GPS signal and see if we can triangulate to get its location?'

'Better than that.' Nick held up a computer printout he was holding. 'Boys in digital forensics have already obliged.'

'And?' she asked impatiently.

'We got a hit. Natalie's phone is travelling north in a vehicle. It's now on the main road that dissects The Wirral.'

'Why didn't you say that?' Ruth groaned.

'I was trying to,' he replied. 'We've got two ARVs heading that way but it's going to take them fifteen minutes. But I think I know where they're going.'

'Okay.'

'I did some digging around on Michael Bradley. Looking at his social media, he virtually lives at Pensby Golf Club. And that's a twenty-minute drive from where we've located Natalie's phone. And it's also the only place I can see where you can land a helicopter.'

'And Michael Bradley owns a helicopter,' Ruth said, thinking out loud. 'So, if he's going to fly his son and Peterson out of the country, that's where he's going to meet them.'

She jumped up and grabbed her jacket. 'What are we waiting for?'

Chapter 48

Fifteen minutes later, Ruth and Nick were speeding north from Llancastell with the blues and twos going. Ruth had every available unit heading for the area of Pensby Golf Club, as well as creating a police road block on the A540 in case they'd got it wrong and Bradley and Peterson were actually heading back to Birkenhead.

Above them, the fading sunshine had been replaced by dark, granite-coloured clouds. The air had become heavy and portentous.

The car's radio crackled. 'Gold Command, this is Control, are you receiving, over?'

Now that Ruth was in total charge of the operation at Pensby Golf Club, she adopted the traditional code name 'Gold Command.'

Ruth took the radio handset. 'Control, this is Gold Command, receiving, go ahead, over.'

'We have an ANPR hit for target vehicle heading north on the A540 at Heswall, over.'

Bingo.

It sounded as if their calculation had been spot on.

'Control, this is Gold Command, received and understood. Thank you, out.'

Nick gave her a knowing look. 'Looks like we guessed right.'

Ruth nodded and then looked up. It felt like the darkness was swallowing the sky above them as the wind began to whip around their car. The storm had finally arrived.

As they passed the turning to Neston, the heavens opened, and the rain began to clatter noisily on the roof. Putting on the windscreen wipers, Nick slowed the car as visibility had suddenly reduced.

'Jesus, this is biblical,' Ruth groaned as she stared ahead and watched the huge raindrops bounce off the road's surface.

Nick looked over at the satnav. 'Two miles, but I can't go any faster.'

Ruth grabbed the radio. 'All units, this is Gold Command, are you receiving, over?'

'GOLD COMMAND, this is Bravo three, we are receiving,' said a deep male voice with a North Wales accent. 'We are now in position at target location but no sign of target vehicle or a helicopter, over.'

'Bravo three, this is Gold Command, received. Our ETA is five minutes, over,' Ruth said as she spotted the sign to *Pensby Golf Course.*

Nick took the turning, still fighting to see where they were going in the torrential rain.

Ruth's radio crackled. 'Gold Command, this is Bravo three, we have visual contact on target vehicle which has just entered the car park at the driving range. We are currently concealed behind the tennis courts but I'm going to send two men into an advanced position, over.'

Ruth assumed that the AFOs were hidden out of sight. 'Gold Command to Bravo three, received and understood, stand by.'

As they entered the golf course, the rain started to ease slightly.

There was a sign with various locations on it. Lowering her window, Ruth peered at it through the rain.

'Tennis courts,' she said, indicating that they needed to take a right.

Nick turned off his headlights. They were now driving just on sidelights so as not to alert anyone to their presence.

A minute later, they pulled up at the rear of the tennis courts where the AFO unit was based. There were several black, armoured BMW X5s parked in a line. This was the usual vehicle for AFOs – or 'shots' as they were colloquially called in the police force.

Getting out of the car, Ruth and Nick noticed a rumble of thunder in the distance.

An officer in full combat equipment approached. He was clad in a black helmet, Perspex goggles, balaclava, Kevlar bulletproof vest, and was carrying a Heckler & Koch G36C assault rifle. The G36C carried a 100-round C-Mag drum magazine and fired at the deadly rate of 750 rounds per minute. In an operation like this, they needed more firepower than the 9mm pistols that they usually carried. They

weren't going to take any risks today. Bradley and Peterson were likely to be

carrying submachine guns, and had already shown they had no regard for human life.

'DI Hunter?' the officer asked quietly as he raised his goggles.

'Sergeant Harris?' Ruth whispered.

SIMON MCCLEAVE

Sergeant Harris – or Bravo three – was in charge of the firearms unit.

'Follow me, ma'am,' he said as he beckoned Ruth and Nick.

They walked away from the tennis courts and up a steep grassy ridge which was now slippery from the rain.

Harris put his hand out to signal for Ruth and Nick to be quiet and stay low.

As they got to the top, Ruth saw the shadowy figures of two AFOs, with Glock machine guns at the ready, hurrying into position about thirty yards from the stationary Range Rover that was in the driving range car park.

The AFOs trained their weapons on the vehicle.

Silence.

Everything was still and quiet.

There was no movement, although Ruth could just make out that there were definitely two people sitting inside the Range Rover.

Suddenly, the sky filled with a rumbling noise.

At first, Ruth assumed that it was the distant rumble of thunder from the storm. However, as the noise got closer, she realised that it had a rhythmic, mechanical quality to it.

Nick pointed skyward. 'Helicopter.'

Glancing at the dark sky above, Ruth saw a white helicopter hone into view. It had to be Michael Bradley.

She grabbed her radio. It was time to make their move against Peterson and Bradley and arrest them before they escaped.

'Gold Command to all units,' she shouted as the noise of the rotor blades got louder and louder. 'Proceed with caution towards suspects in target vehicle, over.'

'Gold Command, received.'

Just as the two AFOs scurried forward to make their

222

move against the Range Rover, the passenger door flew open.

Bradley jumped out holding a Skorpion submachine gun and sprayed bullets in the direction of the approaching officers.

CRACK! CRACK! CRACK!

One of the officers fell to the ground.

Shit!

A stray bullet whistled low over their heads.

'Jesus Christ!' Nick growled as they crouched down.

Ruth looked at Nick in horror as she grabbed the radio again. 'All units. This is Gold Command. Code one. We have an officer down. Repeat, we have an officer down.'

As Bradley continued to fire, the helicopter circled before it descended slowly towards a large piece of flat grass over to the right.

Ruth knew there was nothing they could do until the injured officer was taken to safety.

A flash of lightning lit up the entire sky, illuminating the Snowdonia mountains in the distance behind. The rain's intensity picked up again.

The AFO grabbed his injured colleague by his bullet-proof vest and pulled him back to safety as Bradley continued to fire at them.

The driver's door opened, and Peterson got out. He was also holding a submachine gun at his hip.

Ruth looked at Harris. 'We can't let them get away in that chopper.'

Harris nodded in agreement.

The door to the helicopter opened and Bradley and Peterson moved backwards towards it, firing as they went.

Several of the AFOs returned fire.

Bradley and Peterson reached the helicopter and jumped inside.

The door closed and the whine of the helicopter's engine grew louder and louder.

They're getting away.

'Gold Command to all units,' Ruth bellowed into her radio. 'Disable that helicopter immediately, over.'

Tracer fire came from an AFO positioned over to the left.

It smashed into the helicopter's engine block where the rotor blades were attached, and bright orange sparks flew up into the darkness.

More tracer fire, and the metallic noise of bullets hitting the rotor blades.

Ruth wanted Bradley and Peterson, and whoever was helping them escape, to face justice.

A crunching metallic sound split the air, followed by a deep mechanical growl.

The noise of the engine strained for a few seconds and then diminished.

Ruth looked at Nick.

It sounded as if the helicopter had been damaged enough for it not to be able to take off. Smoke started to billow out of the engine block.

'Gold Command to all units, move in and arrest suspects now,' Ruth shouted.

From out of the darkness, eight AFOs with their Heckler & Koch machine guns trained on the helicopter moved swiftly towards it.

'Armed police!' they screamed. 'Get out and get down on the ground.'

For a moment, Ruth didn't know if Bradley and Peterson were going to try and shoot their way out in a suicidal firefight. She prayed that they could see that they were completely outnumbered and would give themselves up.

After several seconds the doors to the helicopter opened slowly and three men came out with their hands in the air.

'Get down on the ground now!' bellowed an AFO.

Bradley, Peterson, and another man – presumably Michael Bradley – lay down face first on the ground as the AFOs moved in and handcuffed them.

'Thank God,' Ruth sighed as she looked at Nick who blew out his cheeks.

'For a minute there, I thought that was going to go horribly wrong,' Nick admitted.

'Me too.' Ruth felt a growing sense of relief as she watched the men being marched away in handcuffs. 'I know this isn't fair, but I need a very large drink.'

Nick forced a smile. 'And if I wasn't a raging alchy, I'd join you.'

Suddenly, Ruth spotted her phone spring to life.

Whoever it was, now was not the time … until she saw it was the number for the ICU at the hospital.

Her stomach lurched as she moved away to take the call.

'DI Hunter?' she said, feeling physically sick.

'DI Hunter, this is Dr Ross from the ICU.'

'Okay.' Ruth felt panicked.

'I'm very sorry, we did everything we could for Dan but unfortunately he passed away about ten minutes ago.'

Chapter 49

It was 1am and Ruth was sitting in her garden. She had just got home from the hospital. One of the doctors at the ICU explained that they did their best for French but his wounds were too serious for him to survive.

Taking a deep drag on her cigarette, she just couldn't believe that he was gone. It didn't seem real. She could feel her eyes fill with tears. It just felt so terribly unfair.

'Hey,' said a soft voice.

It was Sarah, and she had brought them two large glasses of wine.

Ruth sniffed and wiped her eyes. 'Thanks.'

Sarah leaned in and gave her a comforting hug. 'Hey. I'm so so sorry.'

Ruth nodded as she took a deep breath to try and compose herself. She felt overwhelmed. It had been a long time since she'd lost an officer in the line of duty. The last time, she had lost Sian during an operation at Solace Farm.

'I just can't believe he's gone,' she whispered as she

took the glass of wine and had a long gulp. 'What a terrible, terrible night it's been.'

'If there's anything I can do,' Sarah said, putting a reassuring hand on Ruth's as she sat down opposite.

'Thank you.' Ruth sighed as she reached for her phone. 'I've got to ring Jim. He and Dan were very close. It can't wait until the morning. He's going to be devastated.'

Sarah gave Ruth an empathetic nod.

Ruth rang Garrow's number. It was very late so he might not pick up.

'Boss?' Garrow said in a croaky voice.

'Jim,' Ruth said despondently, 'I've got some very sad news for you.'

Silence.

'Okay,' he replied quietly. He sounded scared.

'Dan was stabbed earlier today at the hospital,' she explained, 'and I'm afraid that his injuries were too serious. He died earlier this evening.'

'What?' Garrow said, as if struggling for breath.

'I'm so sorry, Jim,' Ruth continued, fighting back her own tears. 'I know how close you and Dan were.'

'I can't believe it,' he whispered as if talking to himself.

A few more seconds of silence.

'I wanted to let you know straight away.'

'Yes, of course. Thank you.' Garrow was stunned by the news.

'It's going to be a very difficult time for all of us going forward,' Ruth said. 'Dan was a brilliant police officer and I was incredibly fond of him.'

'Yes,' Garrow said. 'Erm … thank you for taking the time to ring me, boss.'

'Of course. I'll see you in the morning, Jim,' Ruth said sadly as she ended the call.

Sarah gave Ruth an empathetic look. 'That looked very difficult.'

'It was.' Ruth wiped a tear from her eye and then let out an audible sigh. 'Jim and Dan, they were like chalk and cheese … but they were also so very close.'

A figure appeared at the doorway to the kitchen.

It was Daniel.

'Hey, what are you doing up, buster?' Ruth asked, her voice still brittle with emotion.

Daniel pointed up to his bedroom window and then took a few steps onto the patio. 'I could hear you talking.'

Sarah pulled a face. 'Sorry.'

Daniel frowned over at Ruth. He instinctively knew something wasn't quite right. 'Are you okay?'

'No, not really. Something very sad happened at work today.' Then she smiled at him. 'I could do with a hug.'

Daniel scampered across the patio and wrapped his arms around her.

She could smell his clean pyjamas and freshly washed hair.

'Thank you,' she whispered as she hugged him.

Chapter 50

It had been fifteen minutes since Ruth had called Garrow to tell him the news about Dan French. He poured himself another glass of whiskey. He'd promised himself that he wasn't going to drink tonight, but he was devastated. Over the past two years, he and French had gone from partners to close friends. They had made a virtue of their contrasting characters. French called him 'the prof' and teased him for his eccentricities.

What am I going to do without him? Garrow wondered, and felt the overwhelming emotion and shock surge through his whole body.

His eyes filled with tears as he took a long gulp of whiskey and drained the glass. He poured himself another.

Walking down from the kitchen towards the living room, his mind seemed to be peppering him with past images of French and their time together. The highs and the lows.

How is it possible that I won't see him again? That just doesn't feel real.

He wandered over to the record player that had a built-in Bluetooth connection. A combination of the old and new.

Then he took out his phone. He remembered French's favourite band – *Manic Street Preachers.* Scrolling through the playlist on Spotify, he wanted to see if he could find French's favourite song.

Then he saw it. *A Design for Life.*

Pressing an icon on his phone, his stereo burst into life with the opening chords to the song. He remembered French singing his heart out to the song's anthemic chorus. And, of course, French loved the band all the more because they were Welsh.

Cranking up the volume, Garrow drank more whiskey and just stood in the middle of the living room, letting the music and emotions wash over him.

After about a minute, there was a knock at the door.

For a moment, he assumed that it was a neighbour complaining about him playing loud music in the early hours.

Then he had another thought.

Moving swiftly to the front of the living room, he moved the curtain an inch and saw that Lucy Morgan was standing on his doorstep.

Gritting his teeth in fury, he marched to the kitchen, grabbed a large kitchen knife and headed for the front door.

He was drunk, emotional, and out of control – and he didn't care.

Right, I will show you right now …

Pulling the door open angrily, he didn't even stop to ask Lucy what she wanted. He didn't think he'd ever been this angry in his life before and it was frightening.

'Jim?' she said, looking startled.

Instead of replying, he grabbed her by the throat and pushed her back against the exterior wall of his house.

Then he held up the knife.

'Jim, what are you doing?' she exclaimed in terror.

Garrow was just overwhelmed with fury as he held the knife about an inch from her face.

'If you ever come here again. If you ever try to contact me again. If you ever do anything like this again, I will kill you. That is a promise,' he snarled in her face.

'Jesus, Jim, you're choking me,' she gasped.

'I don't care,' he said, keeping the vice-like grip on her throat. 'I've lost everything. And I know where you live. So, if you cross me again, I will hunt you down and I will bury you. Do you understand me?'

Lucy looked at him. There was no clever smirk or knowing smile. Just utter fear.

'Do. You. Understand. Me?' he spat through clenched teeth.

She nodded.

Letting his grip go, he took the knife away from her face, took a step back, and gestured to her car. 'Go on, fuck off. And if I ever see you again, I've told you what is going to happen.'

Garrow could feel his heart hammering against his chest as he watched Lucy clutch her neck and then sprint towards her car.

Chapter 51

The following morning there was a stillness and darkness over the CID office as Ruth did her best to prepare for the morning briefing. They had lost one of their own. It might have sounded corny, but she knew that Llancastell CID was really one big family. They didn't always agree or get on, but because of the job they did, they always had each other's backs. French's death was going to leave a big hole in her team. She had already spoken to the Regional Police Federation and the North Wales Police's chaplain about some kind of service in memory of French in the coming days.

Glancing out, she saw that Kennedy was sitting by her desk completely lost in thought. She looked shattered as if she hadn't slept. Getting up from her seat, Ruth went out of her office, walked slowly over to Kennedy's desk and sat down on the seat next to her.

'Hi Jade,' she said softly, 'how are you doing?'

'Not great.'

'Listen to me,' Ruth said under her breath. 'You have

to let any guilt you have over what happened to Dan go. You left an unconscious suspect with a very experienced police officer because there was a fire out in the corridor. That was the correct thing to have done. Whether or not Sergeant O'Hara should have gone is a different matter, and that will be investigated by the IOPC. But that's not your concern. You did nothing wrong.'

'I wish I could believe that,' she sighed.

Ruth leaned forward and put a reassuring hand on her arm. 'You have to, or this is going to tear you apart.' Then Ruth pointed to her office. 'Any time you need to talk, my door is always open, okay?'

Kennedy nodded.

Ruth got up as she now had the unenviable task of addressing the CID team.

'Good morning, everyone,' she said quietly as she moved to the centre of the room. She could feel her voice wobbling already. She needed to keep it together for the sake of her whole team. 'I know this is going to be a very difficult time for all of us. Dan was a loyal, dedicated police officer. It was my privilege to have worked alongside him. I know that all our thoughts will be with his family, and I'll keep you posted as to when the service of remembrance and funeral will take place.'

She waited for everyone to gather their thoughts. She looked to her left and saw French's empty desk and chair. She could feel the emotion well up inside her.

Then she walked slowly back towards her office and spotted Garrow gazing into space. She would try to grab a moment with him later.

Nick approached just as she got to the door.

She looked at his solemn expression.

'Doesn't feel real, does it?' he said very quietly.

233

She shook her head. 'No. It's like some terrible dream that I'm going to wake up from any minute.'

'I've had a call from the duty solicitor,' Nick explained. 'That scumbag Bradley is ready to be interviewed.'

Chapter 52

Half an hour later, Ruth pressed the button on the recording equipment and stated, 'Interview conducted with Connor Bradley, 9.30am, Interview Room 3, Llancastell Police Station. Present are Connor Bradley, Detective Sergeant Nick Evans, Duty Solicitor Guy Daley, and myself, Detective Inspector Ruth Hunter.'

She looked at Bradley who wore an irritating smirk. This is the man who had murdered French. Part of her wished that the AFOs had shot Bradley and Peterson dead.

Bradley's clothes had been removed for forensic analysis, so he was now dressed in regulation grey sweatshirt and joggers. She had checked the national database, and his DNA and fingerprints were already uploaded from his previous convictions.

Ruth fixed him with an icy stare. 'Connor, do you understand that you are still under arrest for the murders of DC Daniel French, Ian Bellamy, Gary Williams, Natalie Jenkins and Aaron Jenkins?'

He shrugged and smiled. He seemed desperate to let

her know that he just didn't care about what he'd done and who he'd killed.

She took a breath to steady herself. 'I'm going to need a verbal answer from you please. Do you understand that you are under arrest for the charges I've just read out?'

'Yeah,' he replied with a sigh as if this was all a bit tedious for him.

Nick took out his pen and notepad and looked over at him. 'Connor, can you tell us where you were last Monday afternoon?'

Bradley sniffed and rubbed his nose. 'No comment.'

'Did you and Shaun Peterson drive out to Manor Farm on Monday afternoon to see Aaron Jenkins?'

'No comment.'

'Aaron Jenkins was shot by an automatic firearm and killed,' Nick said. 'Is there anything you can tell us about that?'

Bradley sat forward and then looked down at the floor. 'No comment.'

'Aaron Jenkins was manufacturing Skorpion submachine guns with Ian Bellamy and selling them to you and Shaun Peterson, isn't that right?'

Bradley ran his hand through his hair and blew out his cheeks. 'No comment.'

Ruth leaned forward. 'Can you tell us why you shot Aaron dead on Monday afternoon?'

Bradley raised his head slowly and looked over at her.

There was a long silence.

'We didn't,' he said.

Nick looked confused. 'You didn't kill Aaron Jenkins?'

'No,' he laughed. 'You are way off on that, bizzy.'

'Where were you then?'

'Me and Shaun were sitting in a pub in Birkenhead.

The Crown, to be precise. Plenty of people saw us in there. Just ask around.'

This did fit Ruth's concerns about Aaron Jenkins' murder.

She frowned. 'So, you're saying that you had nothing to do with Aaron Jenkins' murder, but you were involved in the others.'

Bradley looked directly at Ruth and gave her a withering look. 'You don't get it, do you?'

'What don't I get, Connor?' she asked, getting irritated by his condescension.

He took a long breath, sat back in his chair, and folded his arms. 'Someone popped Aaron. Had nothing to do with us. But they did a runner with our gun and we wanted it back.'

Ruth assumed that Bradley and Peterson had used the gun in a shooting, and had given it to Aaron to stash. The fact that someone had taken it was very bad news for them in case it fell into the hands of the police. It could be searched for forensics and ballistic matches to other crimes.

'You needed that gun back because you'd used it, didn't you?' Ruth said as she started to piece everything together.

Bradley narrowed his eyes at her but didn't reply.

Nick sniffed and scratched his beard. 'You tortured, kidnapped, and then shot Natalie Jenkins because you thought she'd had something to do with your gun going missing. Or at least you thought she knew where it was. But she didn't, yet you still killed her.'

Bradley smiled. 'No comment.Ruth glanced at Nick. Her instinct that Aaron had been murdered by someone other than Bradley or Peterson was looking correct.

The question now was – who did kill Aaron Jenkins?

Chapter 53

Ruth and Nick walked back into CID still confused by what Bradley had told them. Peterson was being questioned at a police station over in Liverpool as he was facing a string of offences over there on top of the horrific crimes he and Bradley had committed across the border.

'We clearly have Bradley and Peterson for three of our four murders,' Ruth said, thinking out loud.

'Charlie Jenkins?' Nick suggested as a possible suspect.

'He was having an affair with Natalie,' Ruth stated. 'That gives him motive.' She glanced over at Georgie. 'Georgie, has Aaron Jenkins' will arrived yet from the solicitors?'

'Yes, boss.'

'What does it say?' Ruth asked as they approached her desk.

Georgie looked at her computer screen. 'Natalie was the sole beneficiary of Aaron's estate.'

'What about in the event of Natalie's death?' Nick enquired.

'Everything passes to Aaron's brother, Charlie.'

Nick frowned. 'That seems like motive to me. With Aaron out of the way, Charlie gets Natalie and the farm.'

'Except the farm is going bankrupt,' Ruth pointed out.

'Maybe Charlie had no idea about that?' Nick shrugged. 'Natalie said she didn't know. What if there was some kind of residual resentment that Aaron had been left the family farm in his father's will and Charlie had been overlooked?'

'Good point ... and Charlie doesn't have an alibi either.'

'But he does know how to handle a machine gun,' Nick said.

'True,' Ruth conceded, 'but it's been a long time since he has. Maybe that explains it?' Then she looked at him. 'Where are we with that video that Leonard Nevin's grandson filmed?'

'Boys in digital forensics are seeing if they can clean up the image. They're going to contact me as soon as they've got anything.'

Even though there was a mammoth amount of paper-work to do after the events of recent days, they still needed to get to the bottom of Aaron's murder.

'Let's go and have another chat with Charlie Jenkins,' Ruth suggested as she threw the car keys to Nick.

Georgie rolled her eyes at Ruth. 'We know. He's driving and you're smoking,' she joked.

Ruth gave a dry smile. 'Am I that predictable?'

'Yes,' Georgie and Nick said in unison.

As Ruth turned to go, something pinged on Georgie's phone. She looked at it.

'Boss,' she said. 'You owe me a bottle of champagne.'

'Really?' Ruth asked with a frown.

Georgie pointed to her phone. 'I ran those symbols that

were carved into the back of Aaron Jenkins' hand through an AI app on my phone.'

Nick raised an eyebrow. 'And?'

'Apparently, it's Arabic.'

'Arabic?' Ruth furrowed her brow. That didn't make any sense.

Nick gestured to Georgie's phone. 'Does it say what it's Arabic for?'

Georgie peered at the screen. 'Revenge.'

Chapter 54

Ruth and Nick had headed over to Llangollen and were now sitting opposite Charlie Jenkins in the living room of his home. He looked consumed by grief, which wasn't surprising as he'd lost both Aaron and Natalie. Or was he feeling guilt at having killed his brother only to have lost Natalie? It was impossible to tell.

Ruth settled into an armchair. 'There are just a few things that we need to clarify with you, Charlie.'

Nick stood behind the sofa as he surreptitiously looked at some shelves that contained books and framed photographs. He stopped, peered at a book, and then pulled it out.

'You know Arabic?' he asked, looking at the book – *A Guide to the Arabic Language.*

'Sort of.' Charlie looked confused. 'I picked up a bit when I was in Afghanistan. I always thought I'd like to try and learn a bit more. Why d'you ask?'

'No reason.'

Nick then peered closely at a photograph of three soldiers in a frame.

'That's the only photograph of me and my brothers over in Afghanistan,' Charlie explained. 'We were on separate tours, so we only overlapped at Camp Bastion once.'

Nick nodded with an empathetic look.

Ruth leaned forward and looked at Charlie. His eyes were bloodshot, and underneath there were dark bags.

'I can't believe it's just me now,' he whispered as he rubbed his face that now had stubble on it.

'You and Aaron were very close then?' Ruth asked.

'Yes,' Charlie said, nodding slowly.

'Manor Farm was your father's property, wasn't it?'

'Yes.'

'How did you feel when your father left the farm to Aaron and not you?'

Charlie shrugged. 'I was a bit pissed off, but my dad was a very old-fashioned Welsh farmer. It's always been the tradition that the farm passes to the eldest son and so on. Even if there was an older daughter, it would always pass to the son.'

'You weren't jealous of Aaron then?'

'No, of course not.' Charlie gave her a suspicious look. 'I knew that was going to happen since the time I was born. It should have gone to Lee, but he was killed.'

Nick glanced over. 'According to Aaron's will, if he died the farm passed to Natalie.'

'Okay,' Charlie shrugged tetchily. 'I don't understand why you're asking me all this. I've seen the news. You've arrested those two men. They killed Aaron.'

Ruth shook her head. 'Except that we don't think they did.'

Charlie's face dropped. 'What are you talking about?'

'If Aaron died, the farm would pass to Natalie. And you were with Natalie, so effectively you and her would move into Manor Farm,' Ruth said calmly.

'Oh God. You can't think that I'd kill Aaron,' he protested in disbelief. 'He was my brother.'

'But you were sleeping with his wife,' Nick said caustically.

'Piss off,' Charlie snapped.

'And you had no idea that Manor Farm was virtually bankrupt until we told you and Natalie the other day, did you?'

He shook his head. He looked broken.

'You don't have an alibi for the time of Aaron's murder,' Nick said.

'I didn't kill him,' Charlie groaned. 'Why are you saying this? I've lost Aaron and Natalie. Why can't you leave me alone?' He then buried his head in his hands.

Chapter 55

Ruth and Nick were walking across the car park at Llancastell nick as they headed back to CID. They had spent the journey debating Charlie Jenkins' guilt. Nick was convinced he had killed his brother – motive, the affair, the gun, no alibi, and his knowledge of Arabic. Ruth was less certain. Her instinct was that Charlie was telling them the truth.

Nick's phone rang as they got to the top of the stairs.

'DS Evans?' he said as they continued walking.

After a few seconds, he ended the call and looked at Ruth. 'Boys in digital forensics have cleaned up that video that Leonard Nevin's grandson made. They said they've done the best they can with it.'

Ruth pulled a face. It didn't sound hopeful. She pointed over to the building where all the forensic departments were housed.

'Better go and have a look, just in case,' she said.

Five minutes later, they had entered the building and were now sitting with a digital forensics officer. The room was comprised of two rows of state of the art computers facing each other. Above these were black shelves that contained audio and digital tracking machinery, which glowed and made low humming noises.

The officer – thirties, ginger beard, glasses – pointed to the large monitor mounted on the wall.

'Do you want the good news or the bad news?' he asked them as he pushed his glasses up the bridge of his nose.

Ruth rolled her eyes. 'I don't think I can take any more bad news at the moment, if I'm honest.'

'Right,' he said with an uncertain smile as he clicked a button on the computer and brought the video up onto the screen.

There was the shaky footage of Leonard Nevin and his wife Mary sitting on the train, smiling and waving at the phone.

'Give us the good news,' Nick said.

'Good news is that this video has cleaned up much better than I thought it was going to.'

Nick narrowed his eyes. 'And the bad news?'

'As you'll see in a minute, I'm not sure how useful it's going to be when you actually see the shooting. The figures are still pretty blurred.'

'Great,' Ruth muttered irritably under her breath.

'Right, here we go.' He clicked a button and the video began to play in slow motion.

Ruth watched as the footage moved to the right and the field was visible.

The officer paused the image as the two figures came into view.

Then he zoomed in.

'As you can see, these two figures haven't improved very much in quality,' he stated in an apologetic tone. 'I'm sorry it's not more useful.'

Ruth went over to the screen and peered closely. She had spotted something.

Bloody hell!

The figure with the gun wasn't wearing a black base-ball cap at all as they had first suspected.

She glanced at Nick who was staring at the screen.

'That's a motorbike helmet, isn't it?' she asked.

'Yeah, it is,' he agreed.

They looked at each other. And they both knew where they'd seen a helmet exactly like that before.

Haji Rafiq.

Chapter 56

Ruth and Nick marched into CID still trying to fathom if, and why, Haji Rafiq had shot and killed Aaron Jenkins. It didn't make any sense. What was his motive for starters? Had something happened at The Red Lion pub? Did it have something to do with Aaron's affair with Bethan Jones?

'Georgie?' Ruth said as she strode towards her desk. 'Haji Rafiq? Anything on that background check?'

Georgie pulled an apologetic face. 'After everything that's happened, I haven't had a chance to look yet. Sorry, boss.'

'That's fine,' Ruth reassured her, 'but I need you to look now.'

'Of course.' Georgie turned to her computer and started to search.

Nick came to stand next to Ruth. 'It might not be Rafiq,' he suggested.

'Maybe not,' she replied, 'but we have an Arabic symbol and he's Moroccan. He speaks Arabic.'

'So does Charlie Jenkins. Well enough to look up the

symbols for 'revenge',' he reminded her. 'And why would Haji shoot Aaron?'

Ruth raised her shoulders. 'I've no idea.'

'Here we go,' Georgie said as she opened up the background check on Haji Rafiq. A puzzled expression crossed her face as she began to read from the screen. 'That's weird.'

'What is?'

'I thought he said he was Moroccan?'

'He is,' Ruth said, but then realised that they only had his word for that.

'No, he's not. He's an Afghan national. He arrived as a refugee in this country in 2012.'

'What?' Nick shook his head in bewilderment. 'Now I'm really confused. The only connection we have is that Aaron Jenkins served with the Welsh Guards in Afghanistan.'

Then Ruth remembered something. 'In 2013, Aaron Jenkins was investigated for an alleged war crime committed in Afghanistan in 2007. He, Gary Williams and Ian Bellamy were allegedly involved in an unlawful killing of a civilian at a town called Bakhsh Abad in Helmand Province. It never went to trial and the charges were dropped.'

'Okay. But how does that help us?' Nick asked sceptically.

'Bit of a long shot, but maybe the person who was killed was a relative of Haji's? It could explain why the Arabic for 'revenge' was carved into the back of Aaron's hand.'

Chapter 57

Half an hour later, Ruth and Nick arrived at The Red Lion. They were there to arrest Haji on suspicion of the murder of Aaron Jenkins. Even though the pieces seemed to fit together, Ruth still felt that it was a stretch to believe that Haji had managed to track down Aaron, get a job locally, and then wait for the right time to retaliate. But she also knew that some people would go to any lengths to get revenge.

As they walked into the pub, Haji looked at them from where he was standing behind the bar. There must have been something about the way they entered – their faces or body language – but his friendly smile disappeared. He looked spooked.

Suddenly, he dashed along the bar and disappeared through a door.

'Bollocks,' Nick snapped as he ran towards the bar and jumped over it.

Out of the corner of her eye, Ruth glanced out of the window and saw Haji running away across the car park.

She sprinted out through the entrance and took off after him, racing across the car park.

'Stop! Police!' she bellowed.

Haji reached the fence that bordered the car park, climbed over it, and dropped down into a field.

With her arms pumping, Ruth was already breathing hard. If there had been any doubts about Haji's guilt, they had all but gone now that he had done a runner.

Ruth could hear Nick running behind her, but he hadn't caught her up yet.

She climbed over the fence and looked around.

Haji had darted right and was now heading for a steep hill covered in wild grasses.

To her left, barbed wire and an aluminium fence marked out a field where cows were grazing. A couple of them looked at her with disinterest as she sprinted past.

Haji was less than fifty yards away and he was starting to slow as he climbed up the hill.

Ruth was running flat out. Her shoes were beginning to rub against her heels. With the back of her hand, she wiped the sweat from her forehead.

Thirty yards and closing.

Haji glanced back at her anxiously. His escape had slowed to an exhausted walk uphill.

'Stay there, Haji!' she yelled.

Surely he could see that he wasn't going to get away.

Twenty yards.

Ruth was now sucking for air and her lungs were burning.

God, I feel sick.

Haji turned and looked shocked to see that she had virtually caught him up.

'Haji, just stop there!' she gasped. 'You're not going to get away.'

He turned, stumbled, and fell to the ground.

A moment later, Ruth was on him. She grabbed her cuffs, pulled his hands behind his back, and cuffed him.

'Haji Rafiq ...' she puffed out a laboured breath. 'I'm arresting you on suspicion of the murder of Aaron Jenkins. You do not have to say anything, but anything you do say can be used in a court of law.'

Nick arrived and looked down at her.

'Took your time,' she gasped as she stood up. Then she pointed to Haji. 'Right, you can take it from here sergeant before I pass out.'

Chapter 58

Two hours later, Ruth pressed the button on the recording equipment and said, 'Interview conducted with Haji Rafiq, 4.30pm, Interview Room 1, Llancastell Police Station. Present are Haji Rafiq, Detective Sergeant Nick Evans, Duty Solicitor Guy Daley, and myself, Detective Inspector Ruth Hunter.'

Haji looked very frightened – like a lost little boy. Ruth wasn't sure, but she suspected that he wasn't going to go 'no comment' for the interview. He was a million miles from the seasoned criminals that they usually interviewed.

He leaned towards the duty solicitor and spoke quietly with him for about a minute. The solicitor nodded, then turned to Ruth. 'After consultation with my client, we have agreed that he will be putting in a plea of guilty to the charges.'

Phew, Ruth thought with relief. Going to trial was such a huge job for everyone in CID as they had to collate all the evidence and then check and cross-reference it for the Crown Prosecution Service.

'Good,' she said. 'Haji, there are obviously a few things

that we will need to clarify with you in this interview, even though you are entering a guilty plea.'

'Yes,' he said very quietly as he sat forward nervously.

Nick pulled out his pen and moved a pad of A4 paper so that it was in front of him. 'Can you confirm that your full name is Haji Rafiq?'

'Yes.'

'We understand that you are an Afghan national who entered the UK in 2012. Is that correct?'

'Yes.'

'Could you give us your date and place of birth?'

'27th July 1995,' he said softly. 'Bakhsh Abad.'

'And you witnessed British soldiers killing someone in that village in 2007, is that right?' Ruth asked.

Haji's apologetic expression was replaced by one of anger. 'Someone? It was my father. They killed him like a dog. He had his hands up. No guns, nothing. And as he lay injured on the ground, they went over and shot him dead.'

There was silence.

'I'm sorry to hear that,' Ruth said with empathy. There was part of her that felt sorry for him in that moment. 'And you managed to track down the men you knew were responsible for your father's murder?'

'Yes, it was in the paper. It was a war crime. But they didn't even stand trial for it.'

'Can you tell us what happened last Monday at Manor Farm?' Nick asked.

Haji took a deep breath to compose himself. 'I rode over there. I didn't know exactly what I was going to do.'

'You didn't go there to kill Aaron?'

'I don't know. He was very drunk. He thought I was there because I knew him from the pub. Then he opened the gun cabinet and got out this machine gun. He seemed very proud that he had it. Then he asked me if I wanted to hold it. So I took it. And that's when I told him why I was there. To tell him that I'd seen him and his friends murder my father in cold blood. At first, he didn't believe me. And then I made him go into the field. He told me that I didn't have the guts to kill him. That I was just a silly boy.'

'And then what happened?'

'He just kept laughing. Then he pushed me and the gun went off and he ...' Haji looked at the floor. 'I don't even remember pulling the trigger.'

'Where is that gun now?' Ruth asked.

'It's in my flat. I was going to get rid of it but I didn't know how.'

Ruth looked at Nick. They had all they needed for the time being.

'Okay, Haji,' Ruth said calmly. 'You'll be taken from here and remanded in custody. And then tomorrow, you'll be taken to court where a date will be set for your sentencing. Do you understand that?'

Haji nodded sadly. 'Yes.'

Chapter 59

Ten days later

IT WAS MID MORNING, and Ruth and Nick had arrived at St John's Church in Rhosymedre for the memorial service for Dan French. There would be a small family funeral and burial in a couple of weeks. They were both wearing their full police dress uniform. Ruth had forgotten how bloody uncomfortable it was, especially on a hot summer's day.

They began to make their way across the graveyard and walked in silence downhill towards the entrance to the church. The summer air was heavy with a sweet aroma that Ruth inhaled, but she couldn't shake the overwhelming sense of sadness since French had died.

All she could see around her in the graveyard were grey monuments gradually fading into the light. In the near distance was the huge church. Built from local Cefn stone in the 1830s, it was cross-shaped with corner pinnacles.

'I once did a main share at an AA meeting in the room

above this church,' Nick said, breaking the silence. 'It was when I first got sober. My sponsor met me just up there and we walked through the graveyard like we're doing now. He pointed to the graves that surrounded us and asked, 'You know what all these are, don't you?' I didn't know what he was talking about so I shrugged and said 'No.' And he said, 'These are a preview of what happens if you don't keep going to meetings and stay sober.' Sometimes it's a good reminder.'

Ruth nodded. 'You've done so well. I know that I never tell you, but I'm incredibly proud of how you've turned yourself around in the last five years.'

'Thank you,' he said quietly.

As they reached the gravel path, they could see various police officers in full dress uniform talking in sombre tones outside the front of the church.

Georgie approached and gestured to her uniform. 'I don't know how I got this thing on,' she said. She was several months pregnant and starting to show.

'You didn't have to,' Ruth said.

'I wanted to. I know it sounds silly, but I thought I owed it to Dan.'

Garrow came over slowly. He didn't look well. His skin was sallow and his features drawn.

'Hi there,' he said sombrely. 'I spoke to the vicar yesterday and arranged for *A Design for Life* by *Manic Street Preachers* to play as we leave the church today. Dan always loved that song.'

Ruth gave him an empathetic smile and touched his arm for a moment reassuringly. 'Thank you, Jim. That's very thoughtful.'

Nick looked at him. 'And no more hassles from Lucy Morgan?'

Garrow shook his head. 'No, thank God. In fact she

sent me a photograph from Manchester Airport saying that she was moving abroad and starting a new life.'

Ruth sighed. 'That's a big relief.'

Even though Garrow had been standing at a relative distance, she could smell alcohol on his breath. Given that it was 11am, that wasn't a good sign.

She then noticed that everyone was starting to file into the church.

As they turned to go inside, she leaned into Nick and whispered, 'Can you smell booze on Jim's breath?'

Nick gave her a dark look. 'Yeah.'

'We need to keep an eye on that,' she said quietly.

'Don't worry. I'm an expert.'

Chapter 60

The following day was baking hot, and Ruth and Sarah had invited a few people over for a barbeque. The air was still, and thick with the smell of barbeque coals.

Nick and Amanda were sitting on the grass together as Megan ran around in a pink sunhat and sunglasses.

Ruth finished her wine and wondered if she should go and get a top up. As always, she was trying to pace herself. Sarah had put her in charge of the barbeque. They had spent the morning preparing. A table with condiments, salad, napkins and paper plates was on the far side of the patio.

The Bluetooth speaker was playing Ruth's Ibiza chilled playlist via Spotify – *All I Need* by *Air*.

Her thoughts suddenly registered a barbeque that they'd had the previous summer. She could picture Dan French standing in the garden with Sarah that afternoon, drinking a bottle of beer and laughing his head off.

The thought of it caught her by surprise, and a wave of sadness came over her.

'You okay?' Sarah asked, putting her arms around her from behind. 'You look like you've seen a ghost.'

'I'm fine, really,' Ruth said. She wanted to remain upbeat today.

'I think the coals are hot enough to start cooking.'

Ruth turned and smiled at her. 'Oh they are, are they?' Then she gestured to her apron that had a heart shape with the rainbow colours of the pride flag and *Lesbian Chefs Rock, bitch!* printed in white lettering. 'I'm in charge today.'

Sarah kissed her. 'I love it when you're all bossy.'

Ella breezed past. 'Yuck. Get a room,' she joked.

Sarah laughed. 'Any danger of meeting your mystery boyfriend any time soon? Your mother thinks you've invented him to keep her quiet.'

'Oh does she?' Ella said, shaking her head in amusement.

Ruth looked at Sarah with mock indignation. 'Thanks for that.'

'Welcome.' Sarah pointed across the garden. 'Haven't you got some cooking to do, mush?'

'Make a sentence out of 'off' and 'piss',' Ruth joked as she turned and headed over to the barbeque.

Sarah was right. The coals were now white hot.

As she looked up, she saw Nick approaching.

'You haven't heard from Jim, have you?' Ruth asked, as she started to throw burgers onto the grill with a satisfying sizzle.

'No. He definitely said he was coming didn't he?'

'Yeah.'

Nick glanced at his watch. 'I can swing by his place if you're worried? It's only ten minutes away.'

'No it's fine,' Ruth reassured him. 'I'm sure he's fine.'

Chapter 61

Garrow had been sitting in the Cross Foxes' beer garden in Erbistock all afternoon, drinking. It had a beautiful view across the River Dee and the countryside beyond. He had been due to go to a barbeque at Ruth's house just up the road in Bangor-on-Dee, but he was too drunk now. Having popped into the pub for a quick pint on the way, he was now five pints in.

He didn't know what was wrong with him. He felt so completely lost after Dan French's death. On top of that, he had his tribunal with Superintendent Williams hanging over his head. His police federation rep had warned him that he would be lucky to keep his job after the Lucy Morgan fiasco.

What Garrow did know is that the overwhelming sense of dread, anxiety and pain seemed to be numbed by alcohol. He was more than aware that he was self-medicating. Anaesthetising himself to block out the distressing thoughts and emotions that seemed to pervade his every waking minute.

As he finished his pint, he gave a sigh. He knew what

he'd do. He'd drive via an off license on the way home, pick up a bottle of whiskey, and drink the rest of the evening away listening to music. He gave a half-smile at the thought of that.

Getting up from the bench seat that he'd been sitting on, he felt a little unsteady on his feet. His head was thick and fuzzy. What if he got pulled over and breathalysed? He gave a snort. He'd never been pulled over in his life so why would that happen tonight?

Walking up the stone steps, he saw an attractive woman in her 20s coming the other way. They caught each other's eye for just a moment.

She was nice, he thought to himself.

At the back of the pub was another set of stone steps that led to an overflow car park at the top.

The car park was nearly empty as Garrow walked over to his car. The setting sun glimmered orange through the high trees that loomed over him. Then the horrible cawing of a crow from somewhere. He looked up and saw that the branches were littered with crows' nests.

Opening the driver's door, he sat down and shook his head to try and clear it. Then he took a deep breath.

He turned on the ignition. The radio was tuned to BBC Radio 3 and some soft, relaxing classical music was playing.

Vaughan Williams, Garrow thought to himself as he put the car into gear.

Suddenly, a figure appeared from nowhere and stood in front of the car.

It was Lucy Morgan.

Are you bloody joking?

She stared at him with an icy glare.

Rage flowed through him. *Fuck this. I warned you.*

They locked eyes for a second.

Lucy looked at him as if she was daring him to drive off.

He took a lungful of breath and stamped down on the accelerator.

His car lurched forward at speed, ploughing into Lucy and tossing her high into the air.

Glancing back, he saw her lifeless body lying crumpled in a heap over to the side of the car park.

There was no way he was staying to face the consequences of what he'd just done. He needed to get out of there.

Putting the car back into gear, he screeched out of the car park and sped away into the distance.

Enjoy this book?
Get the next book in the series
'The Wirral Killings'

https://www.amazon.co.uk/dp/B0D54F9VCC

https://www.amazon.com/dp/B0D54F9VCC

The Wirral Killings
A Ruth Hunter Crime Thriller #Book 20

FANCY AN EXCITING SUMMER READ?

**THIS IS MY NEW BOOK
'LAST NIGHT IN VILLA LUCIA'**

A TENSE PSYCHOLOGICAL THRILLER

PRE-ORDER 'LAST NIGHT AT VILLA LUCIA'

UK My Book

https:/www.amazon.com/dp/B0CW1KBHTF

THE OPENING CHAPTER TO 'LAST NIGHT AT VILLA LUCIA'

I'm sitting in my favourite spot. I lean forward on the wicker sofa with soft plum-coloured cushions, which is carefully positioned in the shade, just to the left-hand side of my villa.

My villa? It still sounds peculiar and rather grandiose. Even after nearly two years. You'd think I'd have got used to it. I guess it's all part of my imposter syndrome. It's my default position for most things.

The sofa has that little creak as I shift my weight. The tightly wound bamboo readjusting.

And though it's not even 8 a.m., the blazing Tuscan sunshine is already blinding and the air temperature oven hot. A fly buzzes past totally oblivious to what's happened this morning. Or maybe it's a sign. An omen.

I gaze out at the view which I've been looking at every morning for two years. The crest of the hill. The expansive vineyard and then beyond that, sprawling fields, a wood and low rolling hills for as far as the eye can see. It's breathtaking. A spectrum of colour. A landscape speckled by a handful of caramel-brown terracotta roofs of distant villas and farmhouses. Over to my right, an olive grove, golden fields and rows of umbrella-shaped trees. To say that it is idyllic doesn't do it justice.

One of the guests at the villa a few months earlier brought paints and sketch books. He told me about the nineteenth-century Italian artist, Giovanni Fattori, a leading figure of the Macchiaioli. Apparently it referred to a group of Tuscan painters whose use of natural light and colour when painting the landscape of the area was highly influential on the French impressionists. I pretended to be fascinated as he waffled on. And his attempts to capture this view – *my view* – were less than impressive. Better than I could do, granted. But then again, I don't paint anymore, nor would I make a big show of landscape painting if the result was on a par with the work of an eight-year-old. I'm being bitchy. My head is throbbing.

However, this morning, I'm unable to take any of this astonishing view in.

My mind is spinning and out of control.

'My view' has taken on a whole new significance today. I've no idea how all this is going to end. But I am starting to realise that this view may not be 'my view' for very much longer.

I take my Chanel sunglasses which have been pushed up into my hair and pop them on the bridge of my nose. I spotted them on a stall in Portobello Market in Notting Hill about six years ago. The stallholder assured me they were vintage. I thought they looked like the kind of sunglasses I'd seen Brigitte Bardot or Sophia Loren wearing in the seventies and parted with the best part of £200. I've had enough compliments to know that they were worth the investment.

I move a strand of my dirty-blonde hair from my face, tuck it behind my ear and notice that my hand is shaking. It's not surprising after the events of the past half hour. For a moment, I hold my right hand out and watch it quiver. I take a deep breath and try to let it out in a long, slow, controlled stream but the shaking doesn't stop. I need a drink.

By this time of the morning, I would have usually completed my sunrise kundalini yoga class for the guests before making sure that everything is in order for their breakfast. Kiwis, bananas and mangos would have been peeled and chopped. A selection of pastries taken from the freezer to be baked. The coffee machine primed with Melozio pods that are a glorious golden colour. The packet claims they're a harmonious blend of Italian Arabicas with a distinctly sweet note. The split roast adds to the smooth taste and a touch of milk develops a biscuity note.

I'm not sure about any of that. I just know it tastes bloody lovely. I wish that caffeine was my only drug of choice.

And after breakfast is prepared for the guests, I usually wander up to this sofa with my phone, a book and a large glass of cucumber water.

Then it's a ten-minute meditation with a lovely Canadian man called Mike on an app on my phone. He has a comforting, chatty voice that I find very alluring. In fact, until I saw a photo of him, I had imagined him to be a beautiful, dark, handsome man with a beard, in his forties, sitting in white flowing clothes by a lake. Unfortunately, Jeff is in his sixties, with a pointed, weaselly face and glasses. I regret ever looking him up on Google now.

Sometimes, I can find the peace and serenity that I strive for in these guided meditations. Other times, my mind is whirring with anxiety.

And this morning I don't have a glass of cucumber water, a book or my phone.

I'm feeling overwhelmed. Completely overwhelmed by a dread that is making my stomach muscles tighten like a clenched fist. A nasty ball of terror deep inside.

Breathe, Cerys. Just breathe, I tell myself.

So I begin the breathing exercises that I was shown back in those dark days in London. Days when my life was dominated by panic attacks and fear. Before I came to my villa.

In for five, hold for seven, breathe out for eight, I say to myself. *In for five, hold for seven, breathe out for eight.*

It doesn't seem to be working. My pulse is racing.

In for five, hold for seven, breathe out for eight.

I feel like I'm hanging on to my sanity by my fingertips. I close my eyes to steady myself.

In for five, hold for seven, breathe out for eight.

It's no use.

I need to move and not sit still.

I stand up, take a few steps onto the grass and gaze over at the beautiful infinity pool.

I can hardly dare to look – but I force myself.

Oh God.

For a second, I wonder if I had some perverse hallucination when I came out of the villa to lay out guest towels on the sunloungers.

But it's as real as the sun beating down on this terrace.

I go back and sit on the edge of the sofa.

The wind picks up and the air smells of pine.

And then the sound of a police siren fractures the tranquillity.

I wait for them to arrive.

I wonder how this has all happened and how it's all going to end.

Because floating in the middle of my infinity pool, there is a dead body face down in the water.

PRE-ORDER 'LAST NIGHT AT VILLA LUCIA'

https:/www.amazon.co.uk/dp/B0CW1KBHTF
https://www.amazon.com/dp/B0CW1KBHTF

Your FREE book is waiting for you now

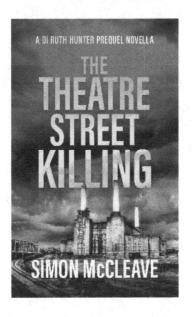

Get your FREE copy of the prequel to
the DI Ruth Hunter Series NOW
http://www.simonmccleave.com/vip-email-club
and join my VIP Email Club

DC RUTH HUNTER SERIES

London, 1997. A series of baffling murders. A web of political corruption. DC Ruth Hunter thinks she has the brutal killer in her sights, but there's one problem. He's a Serbian war criminal who died five years earlier and lies buried in Bosnia.

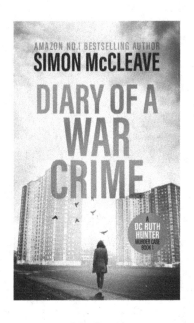

My Book
My Book

AUTHOR'S NOTE

Although this book is very much a work of fiction, it is located in Snowdonia, a spectacular area of North Wales. It is steeped in history and folklore that spans over two thousand years. It is worth mentioning that Llancastell is a fictional town on the eastern edges of Snowdonia. I have made liberal use of artistic licence, names and places have been changed to enhance the pace and substance of the story.

Acknowledgments

I will always be indebted to the people who have made this novel possible.

My mum, Pam, and my stronger half, Nicola, whose initial reaction, ideas and notes on my work I trust implicitly. Carole Kendal for her meticulous proofreading. My designer Stuart Bache for yet another incredible cover design. My superb agent, Millie Hoskins at United Agents, and Dave Gaughran for his invaluable support and advice. And Keira Bowie for her ongoing patience and help.

Printed in the USA
CPSIA information can be obtained
at www.ICGtesting.com
LVHW031210271024
794902LV00015B/258